Mr. Maybe

by

M. Kate Quinn

The Sycamore River Series, Book 2

Mr. Maybe

Cover Art by *Kim Mendoza*

The Wild Rose Press, Inc.
PO Box 708
Adams Basin, NY 14410-0708
Visit us at www.thewildrosepress.com

Publishing History
First Champagne Rose Edition, 2019
Print ISBN 978-1-5092-2764-8
Digital ISBN 978-1-5092-2765-5

The Sycamore River Series, Book 2
Published in the United States of America

He laughed. "So your family's convinced we're a couple. Isn't that what we set out to do?"

"Well, yes."

"Okay, one problem down. Now what's your biggest issue with dancing?"

"No rhythm."

"No rhythm."

"Zilch."

"You like music?"

"Yes."

"Okay, that's a start." He pushed some buttons on the device in his hand. "Let's find something from this century and see what happens."

"Shane, it's no use. I can't."

"Let's have a go at it."

She grabbed her empty wineglass. "I need wine."

In the kitchen she poured herself a half glass of the white zinfandel from the fridge. She took tentative steps to watch Shane as he scrolled through music videos on her television. His black hair curled at his collar, and she wondered what it would feel like in her fingers. *Stop.* She groaned.

Shane turned to the sound. "Hey, I found a good one. Come here."

Just the way he beckoned caused her insides to melt like chocolate on a stove. If she were at all wise, she would listen to that little voice in her head and go lock herself in her room. But she and her glass of wine went to him. Just moments ago she couldn't get her damn feet to move. Now, apparently, they wanted to dance.

Awards and Praise for M. Kate Quinn

SUMMER IRIS (July 2010, The Wild Rose Press) ~ a Golden Quill Award finalist for Best First Book

~

MOONLIGHT AND VIOLET (June 2011, The Wild Rose Press) ~ Winner, Golden Leaf Award for Best Contemporary Novel

~

BROOKSIDE DAISY (February 2012, The Wild Rose Press) ~ a Golden Leaf Award finalist

~

VICTORIA AT SEA (2016) ~ Winner 2017, Heart of Excellence Readers Choice Award

~

"Charming, a great rainy day read."

~Uncaged Book Reviews

Dedication

For my granddaughter, Quinn Mara—
With a big heart filled with kindness,
a spirit that never lets you forget she's in the room,
and the infectious laugh that gets us all going,
she is pure delight.

Chapter One

Swollen gray clouds marched across the sky, and a feisty wind whipped at the leaves on the trees along the river. At eleven in the morning, it was dark as night. Kit Baxter laced up her running shoes anyway. She'd run in a typhoon if it would help her lose the eight pounds she'd put on since The Incident.

It was her day off from her job as the seamstress of Rosie's Bridals, but this morning her boss and best friend, Rylee, had texted that she needed to see her. With the way things were tanking at the shop, Kit worried Rylee was going to announce its closing. That would suck on so many levels, not the least of which was her possible joblessness now that she was a homeowner.

She stepped out into the cool morning, the wind tugging at her ponytail. It had started to rain big fat drops, but so what. She was doing this. The climb up the hill to the road challenged her stamina, made her heart pound. Her calves burned. With each step, she cursed the pints of ice cream she'd ingested over the last few months, the number of chili dogs she'd bought from Gio, the vendor on the square downtown. She had to stop the emotional eating. Chili dogs fixed nothing.

She'd learned that much in the time since The Incident of Christmas Eve. This was June, for God's sake. Yet it was no easy task getting past the betrayal.

Sometimes popping into her head out of nowhere, the Indicent would tease her first with the background elements of that night, the mental image of the festive holiday decorations in Aunt Dee Dee's house, the dining room table set with her good china, a poinsettia-festooned cloth starched stiff. Sometimes she could almost smell the spicy aromas wafting out from Dee Dee's kitchen. But then like the slice of a blade, she'd bleed with the memory of her cousin Co-Co elegantly positioned under the mistletoe dangling above the living room doorway, her slender arms lifted up and laced around Brian's neck. Kit had stood there frozen in place, cemented in the moment, watching that betraying witch kissing *her* Brian, the man she had been convinced might be her one true love. *Ha.* So much for her ability to discern friend from foe, truth from lies, good from no-goddamn good.

Their agonizingly long, passionate kiss broke, and with round-eyed shock they all just stared at each other like a frozen frame of a horror movie. She'd finally darted away from them, and in her black patent-leather flats with the grosgrain bow at the toe, she ran. She ran through the house, dodging the maze of furniture, pushed out the front door, and sped down the driveway. When she'd heard them calling her name, she ran then as she was suddenly running now. With all her might.

The rain came down harder now. She lost her footing and fought to right her stance, slipping on wet gravel, and went down hard on her ass. She tilted her head up toward the rain and let it drench her face. She yelled out loud, droplets falling on her lips and into her mouth. She grumbled in response to the thunder. *Damn this rain, damn these wet clothes, and damn Brian and my lousy cousin.*

She scrambled up on her feet, a crack of lightning making her jump. Shit, this wasn't worth it. She turned to head back home when she heard it. A roaring sound rushed to her ears, followed by an air-sucking whoosh, then cracking and screeching. An inner knowing fought to register in her head despite her attempts to dispel what she already surmised. She ran back down the puddling roadway toward her house, her mind chanting *please, no.*

But at the end of her gravel driveway, the truth mocked her. The massive ancient sycamore she had been warned about at her closing, the mammoth eyesore she was told was her responsibility to remove only she hadn't had the funds, had toppled over from its rotten, scraggly roots. The dead trunk had landed like a targeted missile onto her Honda, crushing the small SUV like a pancake.

Kit was too stunned to move even as the stinging rain pelted her face and attacked her skin like needles. She blinked at the droplets that blurred her eyes like tears, only she was not prone to them. She would not cry and hadn't since Christmas Eve.

A hand gripped her arm, and she sucked in a breath. Her neighbor, the sweet widower who had begun their relationship as a nosy old guy with too much time on his hands but had morphed into a sort of quasi buddy stood there getting rain on his bare scalp.

"Hop." She wrapped her arms around him. He smelled like tobacco, and he wasn't supposed to smoke anymore. She'd yell at him later.

"Come on. Let's get you inside."

Just the authority in his voice comforted her. Her

neighbor's real name was Joe, but because a war injury had left him with a limp, the aging fire captain of the Sycamore River Fire Department was known to everyone in town as "Hop." A take-charge man, he guided her down the driveway, the gravel wet and slippery under their feet. "We need to make a call to the police." She swore like a sailor to which he responded, "Nice mouth."

As they neared the massive tree, her eyes were unable to leave the sight of her ruined vehicle. "Crap," she said. "This is bad." Her mind roiled with what this disaster would cost, all the money she'd need but did not have.

"Come on. Staring at it won't make it go away." He pushed her to her front steps.

In her kitchen he maneuvered her to a chair and gave her shoulders a push. "Sit down."

"Crap, Hop."

"You said that already."

"My car's ruined."

"Okay, stop. Perspective, kiddo. Here's what you have to think—it could be worse. Right? Thank God you weren't in the damn thing. Cars can be replaced."

She snickered. Not if the delight of new homeownership had zapped every last cent she had to her name.

Hop used his cell phone to call the police, and while he talked, her mind played a guessing game on what it could cost to remove the monster tree and the mangled carcass of her car. A few hundred dollars? More? She moaned. Even if she could cough up the money for removal, there was no way she'd be able to buy another car. She had herself to blame. She should have thought it through when she'd decided to omit the comprehensive portion of her insurance policy since the Honda was over ten years old. It had made sense to her at the time, but the thing that made sense today was that she was unequivocally screwed.

Hop came over to the table and sat in the chair across from her. "Okay, they're sending out an officer to do a report for you to send to your insurance company." He reached across the table's surface and patted his thick fingers on her hand with a gentle touch. "Relax. It'll be okay."

"I don't see how."

"What'd I tell you? If you don't believe, you'll never achieve."

His hokey philosophy wasn't worth a damn, so the errant stinging that came to her eyes surprised her. She blinked the sensation away. "You're the best neighbor, Hop. What would I do without you?"

"Ah," he said with a dismissive wave of his hand. "I'm a sucker for your dopey face."

"My face is not dopey."

He chuckled. "You should see it now."

The policeman arrived, and Hop greeted him by his first name, giving a little salute. Hop knew everyone. The officer, a big strapping guy named Leo, took her information and told her a report would be available in a couple of days for her to submit to her insurance company. He explained the town would be expecting the timely removal of the tree and vehicle, or they might issue a summons. Yeah, she was screwed.

She and Hop stood by the kitchen sink, peering out the window to watch Leo drive away. Hop had his hands on his hips, his head tilted at an angle. "Look,

I've got an appointment at the fire house to meet with a new recruit. After that I'm going to call a guy I know about hauling that tree out of here."

"Hold up, Hop. I need to come up with the money first. How much does something like that cost?"

"Couple hundred or so."

Her stomach squeezed. "What happens if I don't have it?"

He held her gaze. "You're going to get charged a fine if you don't move on this."

"But I can't come up with it until maybe the end of the month if I promise myself to eat nothing but peanut butter and jelly for a while."

"Tell you what—I'll take care of it, and you can owe me. Pay me when you can."

"Absolutely not." She shook her head. "No. Are we clear?"

"Then what's your plan B?"

Good question. She knew she couldn't call her mom for a loan. She'd already tapped her mother for help with the closing on this place. But take money from Hop? No. She folded her arms across her chest.

"I'll figure something out, Hop. But I'm going to need some time."

"I'm telling you, Kit, they're going to slap you with a fine, and the longer you wait the bigger the fine."

"It's my property. Maybe I like having a gigantic dead tree in my driveway. That's not a crime."

"It's the law, buttercup."

"That's bullshit."

They stared at each other for a long moment, and then Hop poked a finger in her direction. "I'm not taking no for an answer, so don't try telling me different. You can owe me."

A lump formed in her throat. There was a time to argue and a time to face facts. "I will not take a handout. You get that?"

Hop blew out a lungful of air.

"I mean it, Hop. Either we agree I pay you back or no thank you."

He lifted his mitt-sized hands in surrender. "No handout. Trust me. I won't let you off the hook."

She'd grown up without a father or even a grandfather. This old man was the closest thing she had to a relationship like that. In truth, when she'd first moved into her house, Hop's presence next door felt a bit claustrophobic. The old guy was always looking for a chance to stop by, talk, or take time to visit. She was used to solitude, and there had been a time or two she'd pretended she wasn't home when he'd come knocking, not that she was proud of that.

When she'd lived in her little apartment downtown, her neighbors were as busy with life as she was. She'd relished the alone time, so having Hop next door had taken some getting used to. But he was funny and helpful, and she eventually found herself looking forward to seeing him. The more time she spent with Hop, the more she liked him.

He lived alone, had no kids of his own, which was a shame because in her opinion he'd have been a good dad. They developed a routine, sharing a pot of coffee on Saturday mornings, enjoying a cold beer out on his deck on a warm night. He came over for scrambled eggs sometimes.

His dark eyes, almost black, shiny and bright, were locked on hers. Suddenly, it felt as if she'd disappoint him if she protested his help any further.

"This is beyond kind, Hop. But I will pay you back. In the meantime, if you ever need anything—I mean anything—just ask. I owe you more than whatever that disaster out there is going to cost." She uttered a favorite expletive. "I need to find a way to get a new car."

"That's covered by insurance. You should be okay minus a deductible."

She looked away from his gaze. "Just out of curiosity, what happens if I don't have comprehensive?"

"Tell me you do."

She bit her lower lip. "I did. But now I don't."

"Why, Kit? Why would you drop it?"

"To save some money. The car's ten years old. Since buying this place, all I do is make repairs to stuff around here. You remember last week the showerhead fell off the wall in my bathroom. *Boom.* Right off the damn wall."

"Welcome to the joys of home ownership."

"When I decided to buy the house, things were more lucrative at work. Things changed, and times are tight now." She shook her head. "Just didn't see that coming."

Hop pointed his thumb toward the window. "Well, that baby's a goner. Maybe you can get a good deal on a used car."

"I'm going to have to find a way to earn some extra money. Get a part-time job, maybe."

"Hey," Hop said, eyes alight. "Go on Greg's List. I hear they are supposed to have everything."

"Maybe I'll take in a border. It's Craig's List, by

the way." She suppressed a smile.

"Whatever. That could be your answer."

****

Shane Dugan shook the fire captain's hand, marveling at how the older man had quite a grip for someone in his sixties. His energy was a contradiction to his short, barrel-chested frame and that crooked gait he was quick to tell came from a war injury. Folks called him "Hop" because that's what he did when he walked. He hopped.

"Congratulations, Irish." Captain Monaco's bushy gray mustache quirked when he grinned. He patted Shane on the back. "Hard to believe you're not that skinny kid anymore. You're all grown up, son. Your father would be proud." He poked a finger to Shane's shoulder. "And you grew to be just as ugly as your old man, too, I see."

Shane couldn't wipe the smile off his own face. Hop had been his father's war buddy, his closest friend. Any story his father used to tell about the old days included his friend Hop. Just seeing him felt like family. Shane remembered when Hop would visit; he'd tease Dad about his good looks. The black hair and green eyes and his broad frame were like Dad's, but Shane wasn't a dead ringer. Yet Hop's teasing about it today felt good and connected him to the man even more.

"I can't thank you enough for steering me to Sycamore River. I'm honored to be here."

"Hey, you did it all on your own by acing the civil exam. All I did was let you know we had an opening here in town. We're a good bunch. You'll fit right in."

"Thank you, Hop." He surprised himself at the way

emotion caught in his throat. He coughed. The last thing he needed was for one of his new bosses to think he was a wuss.

"The eight weeks you're in the academy, you'll be spending time here at the station with the guys, learning the ropes. Going on calls as a volunteer and logging in some hours. You'll assist the men and just help out when they need you. Be prepared, though, because you're going to be doing grunt work. Then on August first when all goes well with the academy, you're here full time. Sound good?"

"Sounds great."

Hop patted his swollen belly. "And you'll do some good eating, kid. Trust me. Some of the men can really cook." He let out a low whistle. "Vinny makes carbonara sauce as good as my mother's, God rest her soul. We're a family around here."

Shane's throat clogged again. How long had it been since he had food cooked by his mother or sat down to a meal with family, and what on earth made him think of that now? Mom had died more than twenty years ago. He'd managed to put thoughts of that time into a separate compartment in his head that usually stayed put. But just the mention of home cooking and being with his father's old friend set it free.

After Mom died, Shane and his kid brother, Nick, along with their father had had to fend for themselves. Mealtime had been a joke. They were no cooks, by any means, but somehow they'd managed. Thank God for stovetop macaroni and cheese and hotdogs. English-muffin pizzas had been his specialty.

Just when it felt as if his life was forming a new rhythm, a heart attack took his father a year later, and

Shane, at eighteen, had a thirteen-year-old brother to deal with.

"How's your kid brother? He must be almost thirty. Am I right?"

"Twenty-eight. Nick's doing great. He's a CPA, married and living in Boston."

"You get to see him much?"

"Not really, but he's happy and settled, and that's what matters."

Hop gave his shoulder a squeeze. "You did good by him, Irish."

Shane swallowed the lump that had landed in his throat. He'd had some tough times, but this was his opportunity to fulfill his dream. The idea of being a fireman in a house where all the members got along and where somebody named Vinny made them a sauce—and right now he didn't even know what carbonara was—was pretty damned appealing.

He just wished he could get Dana to be happy for him. In the months they'd been dating, every time he brought up becoming a paid fireman, she did that wrinkle thing with her nose. She orbited within the corporate world. That just wasn't Shane. Every time she suggested he go back and finish college, it was his turn to wrinkle his nose. This was what he wanted.

"How're you doing with the move to town?"

"Good news and not-so-good news. The new apartment building on the green is going to be ready for occupancy in three months. They're already taking applications. I got approved for a one-bedroom. Deposit down and everything."

"Congratulations. That's good, but I guess that leaves you high and dry for three months. You need a bona-fide town address before you start the academy, which is coming up soon."

"Yeah, I start next Monday. Today's already Wednesday. Any chance they'd let me show proof that I'll have a place as of September first and let me slide for a while? I can bunk at my girlfriend's place in Mountain Lakes until then. She's in Europe on business for an extended time."

Hop's mouth twisted into a bunch. "In a perfect world that might work, but not in a small town with a board that loves nothing more than to exert its power. You need a documented address now, a temporary lease agreement you can attach to your paperwork for the place on the green you'll move into come September."

Shane blew out a hiss of air. What the hell was he going to do if he couldn't find a temporary place to live? He'd worked his butt off preparing for the civil service testing, had come in at the top of the candidates. He'd be damned if he'd let a glitch stop him. He was thirty-four years old. He'd been on his own for a long time, had worked in a nowhere job for too long. This was his chance. And, dammit, nothing was going to get in his way.

"I have to find something like today, don't I? I'm desperate."

Hop tilted his head, gave a nod. "Irish, if I could, I'd let you bunk at my house until the apartment is available. But you know how that would look. They don't go for special treatment around here. Especially since I found out the next guy in line after you is a nephew of one of the town muckety-mucks. He would be happy as hell to find a reason to have you bumped out of contention. Government. All rules, no heart."

"Don't even know where to go from here. Knock on doors? Maybe I'll look on Craig's List. There's got to be somebody looking to rent out a room."

Hop's mustache twitched, and his mouth turned into a half smile. "Craig's list. You know something? That's not a bad idea, Irish. Not a bad idea at all."

Chapter Two

Kit was late getting to Rosie's Bridals. The storm had moved past town with the rumble of retreating thunder, as if it were shouting out a goodbye. *Yeah, thanks for nothing.*

She went into the shop through the front door. A year ago Rosie's Bridals would have had a few brides-to-be perusing the dress selections on a Wednesday afternoon, young ladies accompanied by a friend or their mother in search for their dream wedding gowns.

But a lot had happened in a year's time. The shop had suffered a decline in business despite Rylee and Darius' efforts to build clientele. The townies thought the new upscale turnover was ruining everything. It was no secret. All she had to do was look at the storefronts on the square. Gentrification had barreled through Sycamore River's downtown like a steamroller.

Rylee sat at the table, pouring through sample catalogues for the upcoming season. Kit's heart did a flip at her friend's dogged hope. She loved Rylee like a sister, and it hurt that her livelihood was hanging by a thread.

Rylee let go of the book in front of her and came around to greet Kit. "I can't believe what happened with that old tree crushing your car. I'm so glad you're okay."

"Thanks, girl, but yeah, the car is ruined. But thank

God for my neighbor Hop. He's a lifesaver."

"How'd you get here?"

"I ran. The rain stopped, and I needed to blow off some steam. Oh, and it's the price I pay for a winter of gluttony." She gave her midsection a slap.

Rylee's mouth turned into a wry smile. "You're too hard on yourself, my friend."

Kit took a seat at the table. "With no car, I better get used to hoofing it. Seriously, though, I might have to find a part-time job or something to get some extra money for a car."

"I'm sorry I can't offer you more hours. Not these days."

She blew out a whoosh of air. Rylee had her own things to worry about, and she would never want to make her feel bad. "Something will crop up, I'm sure. So what did you want to talk with me about?" Kit's insides squeezed. *Whatever it is, we'll deal with it together.*

"Kit, wipe that look off your face. Rosie's Bridals is not done yet. Granted things are far from wonderful, but we've still got some business coming in. Especially because of your reputation in alterations. Word's out that you work magic."

"I don't know how magical it is, but thank you."

"So here it is. I had to let Freda and Mary Ann go. It killed me to do it. They've been with the store since my grandmother owned the place."

"That's too bad. I'm sorry." Kit did her best to keep her face neutral so as not to betray her concern and disappointment. Freda had been her alterations assistant for the whole time Kit had been on board, and Mary Ann had done sales for years. She'd miss them both.

"So, my friend, for now it's you and me around here." Rylee shook her head. "Think we can do it?"

"I know we can." *I hope we can.* She reached over and squeezed Rylee's hand. "Nothing can stop us. And thank you for telling me in person."

"There's something else."

She didn't like the look on Rylee's face. "Okay. Whatever it is, it'll be fine. Just tell me."

"It's about a phone call I received from a bride-to-be. She wants us to alter a gown that's a family heirloom."

"I can do that." She didn't have a lot of experience with vintage dresses, but she was a quick study. She wouldn't let Rylee sense an iota of hesitation.

"Well, the soon-to-be bride did ask for you specifically, even though I was hedging."

"Hedging? Why? Maybe this could be a whole new angle for the shop. Vintage is on trend. We can advertise that we do custom makeovers of old gowns. I mean, I've only done it a time or two, but the results were wonderful. I'd give it my all. Trust me."

"That could be an idea," Rylee said. "But…"

"But what? Maybe this is a gift dropped into our laps, Ry. This bride and her antique dress could serve as a catalyst for a whole new uptick in business. I hope you told her yes."

"Not yet. I wanted to make sure you were okay with it."

"Of course I'm okay with it."

"But—"

"Stop saying *but*. But what?"

"The bride is your cousin Co-Co."

"What?" Kit's insides cinched like a tourniquet, cutting off her air. She coughed. "Co-Co and Brian are getting married?" Kit had gone out with the guy for nearly a year, and not once would he have even discussed the idea of getting married. One time he didn't call for two days after she'd randomly mentioned her ideas about a country-themed wedding.

Rylee gave her head one quick nod. "I'm going to tell her no."

"The dress!" Kit stood up from the bench. "Is it my grandmother's wedding gown she wants altered?"

"She didn't say."

"It is. It has to be." Kit paced back and forth in front of the worktable. "That bitch." She made a scoffing sound. "I always wanted Gram's dress. She knew that. I used to talk about it when we were growing up. Co-Co doesn't have a sentimental bone in her scrawny body. What a snake."

"I couldn't believe it when she called here," Rylee said. "She's got nerve. I'll say that much."

"Bitch."

Rylee went to the small desk in the corner and picked up the handset of the phone.

"Wait, what are you doing?" Kit charged over to her. "Put the phone down."

"Kit, I'll just tell her we're too busy. It's easier that way."

"No. It's an opportunity for the store, and we can't let it go."

"Don't be crazy."

"I'm serious. This could be the start of a new avenue for us. Remaking vintage gowns. We can do some advertising. Ask Darius. Your dreamboat will know how to spin it."

A smile broke out on Rylee's face. Darius, Rylee's fiancé, had been involved in media and was now campaigning for a town council position. He loved Sycamore River, and he loved Rylee more. He'd have ideas on how to make a new aspect of Rosie's Bridals work to their advantage.

"But I couldn't ask you to deal with your cousin after what you've been through."

"We have to think with our heads. I won't let you turn business away."

"She did mention all her bridesmaids will need dresses. And the mothers of the bride and groom will need gowns as well."

Kit swallowed hard. "So tell the snake yes."

"She and her mother want to come by tomorrow with the dress." She reached a hand to Kit's arm and gave it a squeeze. "Are you sure about this?"

Kit's mouth was dry. This was up there on a list of bad days. "I might need a chili dog for this, but yeah. I'm sure."

Rylee pulled Kit into her arms. "How'd I get so lucky to have you for a friend?"

"Just do me one favor. When my bitch of a cousin's here, make sure you supervise my use of sharp objects."

Kit's cell phone rang, and she pulled the device out of her back pocket. "I swear to God if this is Co-Co, I might have to go visit Gio at the hot-dog cart right now." She connected the call with a zealous swipe without looking at the screen.

"Hey, kiddo."

Her heart warmed as relief washed over her. "Hi,

Hop."

"The tree guy's here now, and later the tow truck's coming to take away the Honda."

"I can't thank you enough, Hop. Seriously, if there's anything I can do for you, just name it."

"Come for dinner at my place tonight. I'll order in. I'll get that eggplant parm you like. There is something I want to talk to you about."

"Okay, sure. I'll bring wine. After this crazy day, I'm going to need some."

Chapter Three

Shane popped open a beer and positioned his laptop on a storage box. He had until the weekend to move out of the apartment. He was mostly done packing, and he'd put his limited selection of furniture into a storage unit. He opened the laptop and fired up the video-call function. He had so much to tell Dana.

"Hey," he said when her face came into view. She looked good, bright-eyed, happy. His mouth curved into an easy grin.

"Hey to you, too." Her voice was light. He loved it when she was upbeat. The lightness wasn't often apparent anymore, and he wished she'd just let herself be fun and easy. The job had done something to her, particularly this stint in Milan. She had taken to saying *ciao* instead of goodbye, and she waved with her fingers facing herself, which made no sense.

"How are you?" he asked.

"Good. Great, actually. *Molto bene.*"

He took a sip of his beer and lifted the bottle in a salute. "I'm celebrating with me, myself, and I tonight. I met with the captain in Sycamore River today now that it's a lock."

She smirked. "Don't you want to know why I'm great?"

"Sure, sure, sorry, yes. Tell me."

"Bellisima Beauty loves our line. Especially the

body sprays that were totally my idea, my baby, if you will." Her voice rose in excitement. She wiggled in her seat. "And guess what?" She didn't wait for him to guess. "They want me to consider coming on board. Can you believe that? Me in Milan? I mean, what kind of dream would that be?"

Shane took another sip and swallowed hard. "What?" A laugh popped out of his mouth. "Wait. Who's Bellisima Beauty again?"

"The cosmetics manufacturer. Like *the* company in Europe. And they'd like nothing more than to steal me away from Sundry Labs. Me!"

"You're not considering it, though, are you?"

Dana's face fell. Her smile disappeared. "I didn't say I was taking the job, Shane."

"Then what are you saying?"

She blew out a breath. "Never mind."

"No, I want to understand. Obviously, it's flattering for them to offer. I get that. But what about your job here, your life here?"

She closed her eyes, then opened them. "I don't know. There's a lot to think about. But finish telling me about you. You said you were celebrating."

"Well, like I said, I met with the fire captain today to go over things. Remember I told you he was a friend of my father's? His name is Joe, but they call him Hop because he limps, remember?"

She wrinkled her nose. "Maybe. But go on."

"He's a great guy." He couldn't help the grin that broke out on his face. "He calls me Irish."

"Irish the Fireman." Her voice was deadpan.

"That's me." He smiled, ignoring her obvious lack of enthusiasm. "I start the academy on Monday, and then the real work begins. I told you I signed the lease for the apartment in the new building on the green, right?"

"Yes. Do you have a view or anything?"

"Nah," he said. "The place is so expensive as it is. I think my place overlooks the parking lot."

"Charming," she said.

"My dilemma now is to find a temporary place for the three months until I get into the new apartment. Scrambling right now with the way this town is growing and apparently the whole world wants in. Everything depends on me having a Sycamore River address."

Dana sighed. "What happens if you don't find a temporary residence?"

He shrugged. "I lose."

She tilted her head at a contemplative angle. "Leave it in fate's hands, I guess. If you can't find a place, maybe it's not meant to be."

He bit the inside of his cheek. His first instinct was to defend his quest. But he didn't want to get into a debate with her tonight. He didn't need a reminder that she was less than thrilled he was becoming a paid fireman.

He spoke his words carefully. "So far fate's been kind."

A wry smile claimed her mouth. "Ever the optimist. Okay, Irish the Fireman, I'm beat. I've got a full roster tomorrow. Meeting with packaging geniuses and the promo team."

"Okay, yeah, sure. I'm going to check out housing possibilities online."

"Good luck." Dana stifled a yawn. "Happy

apartment shopping."

The screen went blank, and Shane stared at it for a long moment. The nearly empty apartment that would no longer be his as of Friday sat silent around him, and he was acutely aware of being alone. The sound of his cell phone startled him, the ring echoing off the walls.

When he saw who it was, he connected the call with a quick swipe of his finger. "Hey, Hop."

"Irish, you find an answer to your housing problem yet?"

"No, but I was just about to peruse the internet."

"Come to my house for dinner tonight. I'm ordering in. You like Italian?"

"Sure, but what's this about?"

"I just might have a good idea that could solve your problem. Seven o'clock. You good?"

"I'll be there. Can I bring anything?"

"An open mind."

Chapter Four

When Kit came home from Rosie's, she marveled how, aside from a smattering of sawdust on the driveway, it was like the morning's nightmare had not happened. God bless Hop. Somehow she'd pay him back every cent.

She kicked off her shoes and padded into her bedroom, where she stripped off her clothes and made a beeline for the shower. When the water was hot enough, she jumped in and let it stream over her from the new showerhead that had cost sixty-five dollars. As much as she wanted to wash away the pressing question that danced around in her head, it was no use. How the hell was she going to find the money for a new car? With luck, she'd find a lease, and all she'd need would be the money down, but even that could be a couple of grand, one at least.

Toweled off, she pulled on a pair of jeans, unsurprised they were a little snug. All this walking would fix that. It had to. And no more chili dogs except for emergencies. She selected a peachy-toned T-shirt from her closet, put on a pair of silver hoop earrings, and slid her feet into her comfy moccasins.

It was too early to head over to Hop's, so she took the opportunity to walk from room to room in her house, the place she'd fallen so in love with she'd had to have it. Today she needed that reminder. It had taken all her savings and a loan from her mom, who had made a point to say that there was no more where that came from.

Mom was on a cruise at the moment with a group of her girlfriends, and Kit didn't even try to report in. Why worry her, and who needed an *I told you so*?

She'd been headstrong about buying the house with its charming loft and the view of the river. She had plans for that loft. She took the staircase up to the space with appealingly wide-planked-pine flooring and the quaint places where eaves cut into the lines of the walls. With the exception of a few storage boxes full of books, the loft was empty now, but someday when she had some money, the plan was to transform the space into a library. She envisioned built-ins for her books and a leather easy chair, maybe a floor lamp with a fringy shade. Already she had decorating magazines with dog-eared pages of ideas for the room. But it would be a long time for those plans to come to fruition. First things first.

The only good thing about the smashing of her car was it had taken the bite out of the news that Co-Co and Brian were getting married. Married! It seemed like a joke, a cruel one. When she and Brian were dating, he'd been one of those guys who never discussed the future. The time she'd dropped a casual inquiry about where they were headed, he'd laughed it off. *Carpe diem, baby.* That was Brian. Live for the moment. Buy the two-hundred-dollar leather boots if you want them, give your credit card a workout, take a trip to Atlantic City for the weekend with your frat brothers, toss away your girlfriend, and marry her goddamn cousin. Seize whatever goddamn notion came into your goddamn head.

She went back downstairs and sat on the refurbished Windsor chair she'd found at the used-furniture store downtown. She shoved with two hands at the recalcitrant window frame until it finally gave way. The day's cooling air rushed in at her, and she closed her eyes to enjoy the way the breeze felt like a caress. She willed the melodic babble of the busy river to quiet her thoughts. Her mind was a tangled maze after this lousy day, but there was no figuring out anything now. She wouldn't solve her money woes tonight, and if she let herself think anymore about the upcoming joke of a wedding of her witch of a cousin, she'd go find the box of Girl Scout cookies she kept in the freezer right where she hid them behind the bag of frozen broccoli florets. So for now, it was her and the river, her reliable friend, and she savored its presence. This place was worth the sacrifice it took to be here.

A few minutes later she went into the kitchen and grabbed the chilled bottle of zinfandel. It was time to go to Hop's.

****

There was a green pickup in Hop's driveway. He hadn't said anyone would be joining them, and Kit was kind of disappointed. She had been hoping to just relax and not have to come up with polite chitchat, not after a day like this.

She knocked on the wooden frame of his screen door and called through the screen. "Knock, knock."

"In the kitchen, kiddo. Come on in."

The door squeaked shut behind her, and Kit meandered down the hallway. She liked Hop's house. The low ceilings and knotty-pine walls gave the interior a honey-like glow. Along the walls hung a haphazard placement of plaques that boasted fire-department achievements. He'd been part of the organization for most of his adult life.

Her favorite, though, was the framed photo of Hop sitting in a banana-yellow kayak on the river. He was a younger man in the picture, and his arms were sinewy and brown from the sun, his chest was broad, and his body lean. He braced the wooden oar crossways in front of him, and with one hand held high, fingers splayed, he waved to the photographer. His face was bright, his smile wide. His wife, Elinore, had taken the photo, he'd explained, and it was taken just before she'd been diagnosed with a deadly form of cancer that eventually stole her away from him. This photo, in Kit's mind, was one of those frozen moments in time where everything was right and perfect. There were no worries, no hint of the looming sadness on their horizon. It made her happy and sad both.

She heard voices, Hop's and another man. She continued down the hallway. Hop sat in the kitchen in his usual seat at the head of the oval golden-pine table, a beer in front of him. On the opposite end sat a younger man with longish dark hair that curled over the neck of his pale-blue T-shirt. He, too, had a beer in one hand and when Hop looked up his guest, turned in her direction. Her heart did a little wiggle, which was ridiculous because excluding Hop, she hated men, all men, not just Brian, although he'd started it.

That disdain for the species did not render her blind. Whoever this was had a nice face, twinkly eyes that appeared light toned, but in the dimness of Hop's kitchen, she couldn't decipher their color. Even from the doorway to the room, she could see he had lashes most women would kill for. And she wouldn't let herself assess the way that blue T-shirt hugged his obvious fitness. Lordy, this guy could almost make a man-hater rethink her conviction.

"Kit, meet the newest member of Sycamore River's Fire Department." Hop gestured to the cute guy. "Shane Dugan. Shane, this is Kit Baxter, the neighbor and friend I was telling you about."

Telling him about? She swallowed the question but allowed her gaze to flash over to Hop. She telepathically sent him a question. *What are you up to, old man?*

"Hi." Shane Dugan stood. He was medium height and solidly built. Inside those faded jeans and T-shirt no doubt was the rugged body of a workman. An errant image zipped through her head of this guy carrying a damsel from a burning building, his strong arms wrapped around her, her weight no test for his physical strength. Lordy, she needed some wine.

"Nice to meet you." She thrust the bottle of zinfandel toward Hop. "Here you go."

He took it from her and pulled a face. "Still can't believe you drink pink wine."

"It's the only pink in my life." She turned to the hot guy at the table. "Not much of a pink fan." He nodded as if he understood, and her face warmed in a blush. *What an idiot thing to say.*

"I hope I have an opener."

"You do, Hop. You took mine."

He laughed. "Wise guy."

Despite herself, she let her gaze flit to Shane. He was grinning. Oh, this fireman had a killer smile. Killer with a capital *K. Get a grip on yourself.*

While Hop rummaged through one of his kitchen drawers, Kit took a seat at the table. It was better than standing there like a fool.

She met Shane's gaze. "So you've joined the fire department."

He gave a nod. "Yes."

"Ta-dah." Hop wielded the wine opener. "I knew it was here somewhere." He grabbed the neck of the wine bottle and began the task of opening it. "Kit, Shane beat out ten other candidates for the only spot. He's one smart guy."

"That's great." She pinned on a courtesy smile, careful that it was not a "you're cute" smile. "Congratulations."

"Thanks. It's what I've always wanted to do."

A voice came from down the hallway. "Romano's."

"Great. Food's here." Hop pulled the cork out with a good tug of the wine opener. "Kit, go let him in."

"Let me get it," Shane said as he rose from his chair and left the room.

She seized the moment to charge over to Hop. Her whisper was hot. "What is this, old man?"

"Whatever do you mean?" His mouth dropped open in mock protest. For effect he put a hand to his chest, as though he were taken aback.

She pointed toward the hallway but did not move her gaze from the man in front of her. "This better not be a setup. I've sworn off men. I hate them."

"Oh, you do not. You hate that moron that two-timed you, that's all."

"And you. Let's not forget you."

"Ah. You love me."

"If this is a setup, I swear I'll kill you."

"Relax, would you? I'm no matchmaker. Besides, I think he said he has a girlfriend."

Her heart thudded. What was wrong with her? This was good news, great actually. The appealing-looking fireman was taken, so the idiot part of her brain could just simmer the hell down and stop cataloging a list of his interesting parts.

"Why were you talking to him about me?"

"Just pour yourself a glass of wine and take a chill pill while you're at it."

She punched Hop in the shoulder. "I'm serious."

"Oh, now I'm scared."

Shane came back into the kitchen, his arms laden with white paper bags turned on their sides. The aroma of basil and oregano wafted through the room.

"Let me go pay this guy." Hop took a step away.

"No, I got it, Hop," Shane said. "My treat."

"Well, now." Hop turned his gaze to Kit. "That's very nice of you, Irish."

She looked away and poured a full measure of zinfandel into her glass. She took a gulp while *Irish* dealt with opening the packages and Hop fisted some silverware from the dish drainer.

Hop carried most of the conversation while they ate, but Shane had an affable, easy way of joining in. She listened while Hop filled the new recruit in on some things about the fire department and the town of Sycamore River.

"Kit here works downtown at Rosie's Bridals. She's the seamstress."

Shane nodded, wiped his mouth with a paper

napkin. "Machine or needle and thread?"

"Both since some jobs require only hand sewing. Beading and lace, things like that."

"You must have a lot of patience."

She flashed a look over to Hop. "Sometimes."

She savored another bite of her meal. Romano's made the best eggplant parmesan, and carbohydrates be damned, she sopped the tomato sauce from her plate with a chunk of fresh italian bread. She would eat salad tomorrow.

"I'm putting this place on speed dial." Shane patted his taut belly. "That could be the best chicken Marsala I've ever had."

"Told you," Hop said.

Shane had opened a second beer and took a good guzzle. He cast his gaze over to Hop before he cleared his throat. Up close this new recruit to the fire department's eyes were a hazel green flecked with gold. Not that she cared one stinking bit.

He cast those greenish eyes on her. "Hop told me about what happened today with the tree and your car. I'm sorry."

Kit took a sip of her wine. She had to do something to break that look he was giving her. Was it pity? A surge of warmth climbed up her face. "Yeah, it was bound to happen because they warned me when I bought the place the tree was dead and had to come down. It's my fault I didn't take care of it."

Hop wadded up his napkin and tossed it onto his dish. "I, uh, was telling Shane here about how you were thinking of a way to supplement your income to, you know, help get another car."

"That's right." She said the words slowly and

narrowed her gaze at the old man. What was he up to?

"Well, Shane has a bit of a predicament himself. Tell her, Irish."

Shane uttered a nervous chuckle and ran a hand through his mop of hair. "First off, Hop sprang this idea on me a little while before you arrived, so it's news to me, but I guess what he was thinking is, actually it's kind of crazy, but—"

"Oh for God's sake, quit dancing." Hop waved a hand toward Shane. "Kit, Shane's got to live in town in order to get the job at the fire department. He's rented an apartment, but it won't be available until September first. He needs a temporary place to rent for three months."

Her mouth went dry. Locking her eyes onto Hop, she said, "Okay."

"It's okay if you're not interested," Shane interjected and then took a slug of his beer.

"Shane's willing to pay you twenty-one hundred up front to rent one room for the three months. That's seven hundred a month for three months."

"I can add, Hop, but no, I don't think so." She looked over to Shane. "I'm sorry you've got this issue, but it's just not doable." She slid her gaze back to Hop, willing him to read the venom in her eyes. Through a clench and a lightness she did not feel, she said, "But thank you for thinking of it."

"Kit, he'd be no trouble. During the day he'll be at the academy, and at night he'll hang out at the firehouse or come here to watch the Mets with me. Right, Irish?"

"Hop, she's not interested. Let's not put her on the spot." He captured her gaze. "It's fine. It was just an idea." His mouth slid into a sheepish half grin. "The idea was a lot to ask."

"You could lease a car tomorrow with two grand," Hop said. "Problem solved."

"Why doesn't Shane stay here with you?"

"Believe me, I'd love the company, but it's against the rules. Did I mention Shane's father was my army buddy? He and I were like this." Hop crossed two fingers. "Brothers almost. This kid here is like a nephew. I'd never steer you wrong, kiddo. I can vouch for this guy all day long."

Kit wanted to kill Hop right here and now. Her face flamed fire, which was handy considering she was flanked by two firemen.

"Think about it," Hop said. "Sleep on it."

"Hop…" Shane shook his head. "I'll find something, really. It's okay." He shrugged. "I kind of thought it was a crazy idea, too."

Hop positioned his hand to the side of his mouth, as if he were telling a secret. "He won't give you any trouble. He has a girlfriend. She lives in France."

"It's Italy. She's on business until sometime after Labor Day." Shane combed his fingers through his hair again. He took a deep breath and exhaled. "Hop, I better go." He turned to Kit. "I'm sorry you got put on the spot like this. Hop meant well. I know he did."

Shane touched her arm. His fingers were warm, and despite her mind's protests, she lifted her head to meet his gaze. His hazel-green eyes glistened, and his mouth curved into a pleasant grin. "Don't be mad at Hop."

Every decision she'd made with regard to men in the last year or so had blown up in her face. She had every reason on the planet to be mad as a hornet at Hop and to storm out of his house. But this codger had been her knight in shining armor more than once since they'd become neighbors. She owed him. And she did have an empty loft and an empty driveway. A perusal of the local newspaper this afternoon let her know the Chevy dealer on Route 10 was holding an early summer special on leases. She cast her gaze over to Shane. He appeared to be a decent guy, and it did seem as if his schedule would keep him out of her hair most of the time. And the fact that she found him physically appealing would fall on deaf hormones because the guy had a girlfriend in Italy. On her life she'd never go near somebody else's man, hot fireman or not. She was nothing like her duplicitous cousin Co-Co. Maybe all this indignation and protestation was like shooting a gift Hop in the mouth.

"Okay, I'll think about it," she and her two glasses of wine said.

Shane's grin was broad. "Seriously?"

"Tomorrow. I'll let you know either way tomorrow. Okay?"

Hop clapped his hands. "I knew you'd come to your senses."

Senses? She was fresh out of them.

Chapter Five

The next day around noon Kit sat at the table in the workroom of Rosie's Bridals with an odiferous, foil-wrapped package in front of her. " 'Buy the house on the river,' I said." She unfolded the foil. The heat from the chili dog wafted with succulent aroma to her nose. " 'It'll be fun to own a fixer-upper. Fun,' I said. So much fun."

Rylee looked up from a carton of supplies she was unloading. "I can smell you a mile away."

"I have issues." Kit lifted the pungent sandwich to her mouth. "Going straight to hell." She took a big bite.

"Is this about the lack of money or your cousin coming to the shop today?"

"Both." She swallowed. "And don't forget the fireman factor."

"Are you leaning toward renting him the loft?"

"I don't know. What would you do, Rylee? I mean, I know nothing about the guy. He could be an axe murderer. Firemen have axes."

"Based on what you've said, he comes highly recommended by your friend Hop. I don't think Hop would steer you wrong. Besides, you said this fireman seemed nice."

She took another bite and mulled her friend's words while she chewed. "Yeah, but what do I know about judging men? I thought Brian was *the one*."

A female voice came from out in the main showroom. "Hello," the voice called with a trail of the *o* sound. "Anybody home?"

Kit knew that childish singsong cadence. Her cousin Co-Co. A cringe climbed up her spine as if it were wearing combat boots. She pulled her gaze over to Rylee and mouthed a *stab me* while jerking her index finger toward her eye several times.

"You want me to go tell her we need to reschedule," Rylee whispered.

Kit let out a hissing breath. She gulped half a bottle of spring water. "No." She took another sip. "There's no avoiding her." She dabbed a napkin on her mouth and stood up from the worktable. "Aside from this being an opportunity for the store, I don't want anybody in my family thinking I'm upset about this stupid wedding. Any misstep on my part would be taken as sour grapes. I wouldn't give that one out there the satisfaction."

"Okay, but just say the word, and we pull the plug on this deal."

Kit produced a smile that felt too big for her face. "I've got this." Then she belched.

****

When Kit emerged from the back room, she cast her gaze on the two of them, Co-Co along with her mother, Kit's Aunt Dee Dee. Co-Co had a white vinyl garment bag slung over one arm. The mother and daughter duo broke out in grins as they stood there with their same strategic blonde highlighting sprinkled through their matching shoulder-length bobs. They might have been wearing the same coral-toned lip gloss, too. Kit manufactured a happy face while her belly tumbled around with too much hot dog and chili.

"There she is." Aunt Dee Dee came up to Kit and wrapped her in a strong hug.

She smelled of potpourri or a funeral parlor. Kit couldn't tell. But the pungent aroma of floral overload wreaked havoc in her already-uneasy stomach. She swallowed hard. A bead of sweat broke out at her hairline.

With a look of appall, Aunt Dee Dee waved a hand in front of her face. "Have we interrupted your lunch, dear?"

"No, I was through."

Co-Co pulled a face. "What did you have?"

Kit lifted her chin. "A chili dog."

"Oh my." Aunt Dee Dee placed a hand to her chest. Her mascara-laden lashes fluttered like spastic spiders as she cast a gaze down Kit's form. "Salads, dear. They're a much better choice for lunch."

"Kale," Co-Co added with an encouraging nod. "You'll love kale once you get used to it. Chop it, though, so you don't choke."

Kit coughed over the sound of the rumbling in her stomach. She had to get this over with. She pointed to the garment bag. "Yes, so is this it?"

Dee Dee grinned, and Kit couldn't help noticing how her coral lipstick had bled into the small crevices around her mouth, almost like a starburst around her pie hole. It wasn't as if she didn't appreciate Aunt Dee Dee. She was Mom's only sister, younger by two years. But all during her growing up, Dee Dee had been a pain in the ass and blind as a damn bat when it came to her precious little Co-Co and her deviousness.

Kit's mom and Dee Dee were both widowed now,

and they couldn't be living more diverse lives in their retirement years. Dee Dee lived vicariously through her only child, hovering like a helicopter around Co-Co as much as when she was a kid growing up.

Kit's mom, Regina, was out living one adventure after the other. She was rarely home at her little condo at an active adult community in Essex County. Currently, she was on a two-week mahjong cruise in the Western Caribbean. Did Mom even know about the engagement and the plans for Gram's wedding gown?

"I have some ideas for making changes to Grammy's dress." Co-Co made her glossy mouth bunch into an exaggerated pout. "Just a couple of teeny-tiny ones."

Kit's stomach twirled like a carnival ride. She watched Co-Co with her french manicure and that dazzling diamond on her finger unzip the garment bag to reveal the vintage wedding gown, one Kit recognized very well. The pearly-toned, bias-cut satin, the beading on the pointed sleeves on the gown she herself had hoped to wear one day. Being six months older than Co-Co, she was the one in line for Gram's gown. But that would require a groom, and Co-Co had him. She had the guy, and she had the dress. Kit had a stomach roiling with a poor lunch decision.

Kit eyed the subtle lines of the dress, its timelessness. The old photograph of her grandmother on her wedding day that she kept in a frame on her dresser came to mind. Gram's hair was prim in that sausage-roll style, her padded shoulders sharp and elegant. Tucked in the side of the frame was another snapshot of her grandmother, one Kit's own mom had given to her after she'd cleaned her attic. Gram was alone in the photo and bore the most magnificent smile she'd ever worn. In the black-and-white photo, Gram's dress—maybe an Easter outfit, Kit didn't know—appeared a pale gray. But Mom had told her it had been pearly-pink sateen, which she couldn't fathom. Kit just didn't get pink, too girly maybe, or too fussy. The only pink she liked was a nice cold glass of zinfandel. But she did like the sparkly rhinestone buckle on the belt. That had been a nice touch and so much like Gram. Always with a hint of whimsy. She'd so loved Gram.

Gram had told Kit to choose well when it came to her wedding dress and to the husband she would wear it for, and like that, she thought of Brian.

Her mind replayed the moment when Brian had finally caught up to her when she'd lost steam running from him Christmas Eve. Her feet in the ruined patent-leather flats were frozen and numb, and she had wished the painful deadness had climbed up to her heart. His voice was alive in her mind, his apologizing a million times, telling her he and Co-Co *just couldn't help themselves* because they were *destined* for each other. Even as she tried to banish the thoughts, her insides went round and round, making noises like rocks in a dryer.

"Will you help me make Grammy's dress perfect for my wedding?" Co-Co bit her lower lip. "Please, Kitty-Cat? This is the most important thing in my life."

Kitty-Cat. She hated that nickname, hated that this cousin of hers had snatched up a family heirloom to make it her own. The dress was her *most important thing*? What would this little twit do if a one-hundred-year-old tree had slammed on top of her car and she had no money to rectify the situation?

How was she supposed to respond to this girl? Sure, go ahead, take the guy, and take the dress? Before Kit could say a thing, though, she reached down for the wastebasket by the desk and emptied herself of too much chili dog in one awful wretch.

Chapter Six

"Are you sure you're okay?" Aunt Dee Dee asked a while later when Kit emerged from the ladies' room in a minty cloud after some serious gargling. "We can come back another time."

"Mother, no, we can't. We're in a time crunch."

Kit's stomach was empty, but her mind was full. She wanted to tell Co-Co she could take that old dress and that new solitaire diamond ring with the baguettes and march her skinny ass out of Rosie's Bridals. She'd deal with the fallout when it made its way through the family grapevine.

But out of the corner of her eye, she spotted Rylee as she lovingly positioned a shipment of tiaras in a display case. This shop meant everything to Rylee. It was her legacy, and she'd worked so hard to help make it succeed. Kit couldn't be the one to turn away any business.

"I'm fine." Kit smoothed her hands down her front. "Let's do this. Co-Co, did you say that you'll be having your bridesmaids coming to Rosie's for their dresses?"

"Yes! And we'd like to find dresses that will complement mine, of course."

"Of course."

"I'll make an appointment today for the girls. I have ten bridesmaids, well, nine plus one junior bridesmaid, Cousin Paul's daughter, Abigail."

Oh for God's sake.

"Okay, so tell me what you have in mind for the alterations." Kit smoothed her hand over the fabric of the dress. She did her best to detach from its loveliness, its history. But her fingers savored the nub of each bead as her touch ran over the intricacies of the pattern.

"I was thinking of lopping off the arms maybe." Co-Co tilted her head. "Making it strapless if we could?"

Sharp filaments of anger sliced through her, and heat flooded her cheeks. She clenched her fists, feeling the bite of her fingernails digging into the flesh of her palms. "You what?"

Co-Co held up one of the sleeves of the dress as if it were a fish she'd caught that had just died in the bucket. "I can't do long sleeves for an August wedding. Not going to sweat like a pig on my own wedding day."

"You can't be serious."

"Why?"

Kit bit back an expletive. "Not happening."

Co-Co dropped the sleeve and folded her arms. "Mother, you see? What did I tell you? She's still mad at me."

"Girls." Aunt Dee Dee touched a hand to each of their arms. "Let's remember we're family no matter what. Kit, honey, we came to you because you're the best, of course. But also, if you help with the, um, redesigning of Grammy's gown, then it's like you've shared in its legacy as well. See? It's perfect."

"I'm not chopping off the sleeves," Kit said. "I draw the line."

"But…"

"No," Kit said. "I'll tailor Gram's dress to your

body. I'll fix the beading, replace any missing stones. But I will not, cannot take scissors to that dress."

Co-Co pursed her lips. "You're just saying that to be mean."

"You're ridiculous." She turned to walk away from them.

"Wait," Aunt Dee Dee called. "Kit, dear, come on, wait."

She turned back to them.

Aunt Dee Dee put her hands together as if in prayer. She looked to her daughter. "Co-Co, honey, maybe Kit's right."

"What?"

Kit half expected Co-Co to pull one of her fits like in the good old days when they were in grammar school. Like the time she locked herself in the coat closet in fourth grade when she'd lost out on the lead in their end-of-year play. Kit had been chosen as the damned narrator, as she had every year since first grade, and nobody saw her hiding among the windbreakers and bookbags.

"Look." She closed the distance between them. "If Gram's gown isn't the vision you had in mind, maybe we can show you another dress that better suits you. We have so many great designer samples—"

"No, no. You're not talking me out of the dress. Nice try." Co-Co folded her arms across her chest. "Fine. We'll keep the sleeves. Just make me look spectacular in it. That's all I want."

How could she share DNA with this twit? She needed to quell the fire in her veins. As much as it hurt that Co-Co had Gram's dress in her bony-fingered clutches, Kit had bigger things to worry about.

When Aunt Dee Dee meandered over to a rack of mother-of-the-bride dresses, Co-Co took the opportunity to sidle up to Kit. "You're okay about all this, aren't you, Kitty-Cat? I mean, you and me, we're fine now, aren't we?"

Kit blew out a minty-mouthwashed breath. "Stop beating a dead horse. I'm over it."

"I just don't want it to be awkward for you, you know, attending the wedding festivities alone and everything."

Kit pointed to one of the dressing cubicles. "Take the dress in there and try it on so I can see what we're dealing with."

Co-Co came in close for a stage whisper. "Lola's groomer is single. I think you might like him, and you'll get used to his glass eye. I won't even tell you which one it is. You'll never guess."

Lola was Co-Co's spasmodic Something-poo, and Kit was not at all interested in meeting her faux-eyed groomer. She tamped down the niggle of anger that rose in her veins. "No, thanks. Go try on the dress."

"I just hate that you're alone."

"I'm not, okay? Happy?"

A smile broke out across Co-Co's face. "You're seeing someone?" She whipped around. "Mother, Kit's dating."

Kit wasn't prone to lying, but somehow this one tumbled out of her mouth, and there was no pulling it back. She'd deal with it later.

"Oh, do tell," Aunt Dee Dee cooed as she closed the gap between them, her hands waving in the air as if she were about to take flight.

"Not now."

"Come on," Co-Co urged. "Just a tidbit. What's his name?"

Kit pulled open the door to the dressing cubicle. "Change, Co-Co. I mean it."

"Fine, but just so you know, I'm counting this as a preliminary fitting because I'm bloated this week. I thought I'd come back next week for any adjustments. That good with you, Kitty-Cat?"

"No can do." There was no way Kit was going to accommodate her cousin's tragedy of premenstrual bloat. Co-Co and her cycle could just deal with it.

"Why not?"

Co-Co had the simpering whine of a toddler. Maybe she was teething. And she didn't need to know that the lessened client load around here gave Kit's schedule a lot of leeway these days.

"We're booked next week, Co-Co. As it is, count yourself lucky I was even able to squeeze you in today. Now, are you going to go put on the dress or what?"

"You're being deliberately difficult."

Did she stamp her foot? Kit sucked in a breath to keep from calling her a body part. She thrust her arm toward a dressing room. "You can either go in there and put on the gown, or you can go home. I don't care. But do one of those things now."

The little bell that hung above the front entry jangled, and Shane Dugan strode in. The catgut of nerves in Kit's midsection tightened its gird. He wore a fire academy T-shirt that clung to his muscles. His black hair looked damp and had been combed back over his head, leaving his pleasant face more exposed, open, his smile eye catching. *Lordy.* He was a fine specimen of a firefighter. Something inside her did a little somersault, her pheromones ignoring totally that she was the self-appointed president of the man-haters club.

Co-Co unfolded her arms from her chest, casually put a hand to her blonde bob, and gave it a tussle. In Co-Co speak that was a loud *Notice me.*

Shane latched his mottled-green gaze on to Kit, and his full mouth broke into a grin. Despite herself, her heart did a wiggle.

"Hi," he said.

"Hi."

"I see you're busy." He cast a glance toward Co-Co. "I was hoping you had a few minutes to talk."

Kit watched Co-Co's gaze move back and forth between them in rapid succession. She was a walking, talking slot machine. "Sure." She bit her lip. "Just give me a sec." She slid her gaze over to Co-Co. "Are we done here, or are you going to try on the dress?"

"Fine." Co-Co's tone changed to that teasing lilt she saved for each and every man on the planet. "I'll ignore the grumpy pill you took this morning, and we'll do it your way, Kit. But before I change into the dress, are you going to introduce me to your friend?"

"Nope. Go change."

Co-Co looked around Kit and waved her fingers. "Hi, I'm Co-Co, Kit's cousin."

Aunt Dee Dee sidled up beside Kit and lifted a coy shoulder. "Who have we here? I'm Kit's aunt and the mother of the bride here."

"Pleased to meet you."

Co-Co came close. "And you're?"

"Shane." He looked over to Kit, one eyebrow quirked upward, giving him a look that Kit decided meant he wasn't buying Co-Co's saccharine persona. Even though she hated men, right at the moment she kind of liked Shane Dugan.

"I can come back," he said. "I wanted to get your thoughts about my moving in."

While Kit's heart plummeted to her feet, Co-Co coughed and slapped a hand to her chest. "Are you her new man? Oh my God, and you're moving in together?" She sounded as if she'd sucked helium.

Kit didn't answer but instead prayed for a bolt of lightning with good aim. Considering it was one of those blue-sky, yellow-ball-of-sunshine kind of days, the chances were slim.

"Is that what I'm hearing? You two are a couple?" Aunt Dee Dee slapped a hand to her chest, and the valise-sized purse over her arm went swinging.

"My next appointment is due in fifteen minutes." It was another lie, but this was a desperate situation. She needed a second to think her way out of this. "We have to do this now or reschedule, and like I told you, I'm pretty much booked for the foreseeable future." Lie number three. She was going to hell.

"All right, all right," Co-Co said. She grabbed her mother by the arm. "Mommy, come on. You need to help me." She cast her doe-eyed gaze on Shane. "But don't go anywhere, you. I want to hear everything about you two."

Co-Co and Aunt Dee Dee disappeared into a dressing room, and when the door had sufficiently clicked shut, Kit gave Shane a poke in the shoulder, one hell of a taut shoulder. "Come here." Her whisper was a hot rasp. She marched toward the bank of windows at the front of the store. "We need to talk."

The sunlight coming in through the windows brought out the multiple flecks of gold in his eyes, and she did her best to ignore their appeal. She swallowed hard. "Shane." Her eyes flashed to the door to the dressing room. "Here's the thing." She pinned his gaze. "That's my cousin and my aunt in there and…"

"I think I know this story," he whispered back. He leaned in close. He smelled spicy, like cloves. "Hop mentioned something."

"Oh, did he? Nice. I'll kill him later, but for now listen up." She took a breath. "So you know she's marrying my ex-boyfriend." Shane nodded. "Well, she was just saying how terrible it is that I'll be alone for all the wedding activities, and God only knows what that means, and I kind of stretched the truth, okay? No, I lied, okay? I'm not proud of it, but yeah. I sort of intimated that I have a boyfriend. And then you walked in the door. She's assuming you and I are, you know, a couple, especially since you said you wanted to talk about moving in."

"Oh boy. I'm sorry. That didn't help the situation, did it?"

"No." She watched the brass doorknob of the dressing room. "Here's the deal, Shane. I know you have a girlfriend in what was it, France or something?"

"Italy."

"Yes. Italy. But for now, could you just go along with it? The wedding's August fourth. Maybe you wouldn't even have to attend the spectacle with me. I could say you had to work. Something was on fire maybe. If you help me out, the loft is yours. For the two grand up front, of course."

The door to the dressing room burst open, and

Aunt Dee Dee came out first, her hands clasped in front of her. "Oh, Kitty-Cat, wait till you see how my baby looks in Grammy's gown."

She latched on to Shane's gaze. This fireman owed her nothing, but she needed him to take her offer. She couldn't even think about what that meant. For now, all she worried about was that two-timing cousin of hers emerging from the dressing room wearing Gram's wedding gown.

His green eyes flashed over to the scene at the dressing room; Co-Co had stepped out of the cubicle, Aunt Dee Dee audibly sucking in her breath. He fixed his gaze back on to her. "Deal," he whispered.

"Thank you, thank you." She had pulled a nice-enough, unassuming guy she barely knew into her web of lies. She was shameless.

Co-Co looked stunning in Gram's gown. Even Kit had to admit it. The gown was at least two sizes too large, but with Aunt Dee Dee holding the excess in her fist from behind, it was apparent that when Kit did the alterations, Co-Co would make for a beautiful bride.

"I've got my work cut out for me, huh." Kit came up and nudged Aunt Dee Dee's hand from the fabric. She pushed at Co-Co's shoulder. "Turn around."

Co-Co gingerly made a slow full circle and stood facing Kit and Shane. She pulled bunches of the fabric into her hands, stepped over to Shane, and gave him a coy look. "Hey, you," she cooed. "You have no idea how happy I am to meet you." She lifted her shoulders in delight. "Mother, aren't they adorable together?"

"I can't believe it." Aunt Dee Dee's voice rose high, as though it were so farfetched Kit could have found a man. She licked her lips, collected herself, and extended her hand like a debutant. "I'm delighted."

Shane promptly accepted the handshake.

"Welcome to the family."

Kit pinched the space between her eyes where a headache had begun to throb into the beat of a one-word chant going on in her head—*liar, liar, liar.*

Co-Co clapped her hands. "I guess we'll all be seeing you at all the wedding events." She turned to Kit. "Saturday! Don't forget! The whole family can meet your new man at Mom's dinner party on Saturday."

Saturday's dinner party. Crapola. She'd forgotten all about it. Kit met Shane's gaze and tried to convey an apology.

A relentless Co-Co leaned in close. "Touchy subject, I know, but I'm sure you're aware of the circumstances." She pulled her mouth downward into an exaggerated frown. Just as quickly her coral-slick mouth sprang free into a grin to rival a gussied-up jack-o'-lantern. "But this changes everything. Brian is going to be so relieved. I mean happy, yes, happy to hear the news."

"Come on," Kit said. "Let's get you pinned." She tapped a finger onto the face of her watch. "Chop-chop."

"I, uh, have to get going anyway," Shane said. He met her gaze. "We'll talk later, then. Okay?"

"Sure, yes," she said. "Uh, Shane." For effect, she rubbed her hand up and down his upper arm. Quite the upper arm. "Have a good day, um, babe."

The awkwardness cut off her air. Her lungs were filled with cement now, too. And while she suffered to breathe, he wrapped one of his big arms around her shoulders and gave her a squeeze. She peered up at his face, her mouth open, but she was too stunned to speak. Then just when she was sure this could not be happening, Shane Dugan kissed her on the temple.

"See you later, honey." He flashed a smile to Co-Co and her mother. "Have a nice day, ladies."

"The pleasure was all ours!" Co-Co gushed, and Aunt Dee Dee smiled like a loon.

Kit's eyes followed him as he left the shop while she breathed in and out. He opened the door to his green truck and lifted his gaze. He smiled at her through the front window, and then he winked.

Chapter Seven

While Kit gathered her measuring equipment and her box of pins, readying to cinch Gram's dress around Co-Co's scrawny body, Co-Co droned on about Shane. "I can't believe you've been keeping that boyfriend of yours a secret. When were you going to let people know?"

Kit swallowed hard. "I guess today."

Co-Co threw her arms around her. "Yay for you, Kitty-Cat. The whole family is going to be so happy for you. And Brian, too. He's going to be so glad."

Oh God. What had she and this fireman done? Maybe she'd have been better off with an axe murderer. This was going to flood the family's pipeline like a spark to a gas can. Every relative near and far would learn this *fake news* before day's end. That was how her family worked. And her mother! Oh God. How was she supposed to explain this to her mother? She had until Saturday to explain this away. Right now, though, she wanted a vat of rocky road ice cream and a shovel.

Co-Co interrupted the flash of thoughts going on in her head. "So tell me, tell me, how did you meet him?"

"I'm serious, Co-Co. Stand still unless you want to be a human pincushion."

"Okay, okay, but I've got lots of questions…"

"Later. Now shut up and let me do my job."

Co-Co's cell phone sounded. "Wait," she said,

rummaging through her purse. "I have to get this. I'm waiting for a call from the travel agent."

Kit groaned. This was like trying to train a puppy. She snapped the fabric measuring tape held taunt between her hands while her cousin yapped on about a trip to some luxurious island she insisted had to have personal hammocks. "No time for this," she said, and Co-Co merely held up her index finger. Kit stormed out of the dressing room.

"Everything okay?" Aunt Dee Dee asked from where she sat like Miss Muffet on a tufted cushion outside the bank of dressing cubicles.

"She's on the phone with her travel agent."

Rylee had just finished up with a bride-to-be and her mother, the older woman having come to the weighty decision to go with a teal-toned, knee-length, mother-of-the-bride dress rather than an eggplant-colored chiffon. She pinned Kit's gaze and motioned toward the stockroom. "Can I see you for a moment?"

"Sure." Kit turned to her aunt and pointed toward Co-Co, who had her cell phone pressed to her face and was rattling on about honeymoon details. "Tell her she's got five minutes."

In the workroom Rylee put her hands to the sides of her face. "Kit, did I just see what I think I saw?"

"This is insane. I'm insane." Kit's voice was a rasp of incredulity. She couldn't help it. She felt as if she'd been hit by a truck, sideswiped by a pair of lips to her temple.

"I thought I was seeing things. What the heck was that all about?"

"Keep your voice down. My cousin's in there champing at the bit for details."

"What details? I'm so confused." Rylee shook her head. "Why'd that guy put his arm around you, and did he give you a smack?"

"He's my boyfriend."

Rylee laughed. "No, really."

"Yeah, I am officially living a lie."

She explained how it went down, and the entire time Rylee was slack jawed. By the time Kit was done talking, she'd worked herself up again. Her heart flew around in her chest, looking for a way to escape.

"This is a disaster." Kit began to pace.

"Maybe."

"What do you mean *maybe*? It's a total horror show. When I tell everyone that the guy's just renting my loft, they're going to laugh their asses off about what a pathetic loser I am. Or they'll want to lock me up for being delusional. I think I need to move. Someplace far. What's Oregon like?"

"Kit, I kind of like the fact this fireman of yours is willing to play along."

"He's not mine. I've rented him. He has a girlfriend, for God's sake. Wouldn't she love to hear how her boyfriend likes to play along?" She groaned. "Hawaii. You can't get there by car. I should move to Hawaii. Has the volcano calmed down? Who cares? I'm my own volcano."

"Okay, stop and listen, friend. Think about it for a second. If this Shane guy is willing to assume the role of your boyfriend for a while, I say why not? Think about the grief it's going to save you. Weren't you just telling me how you're dreading going to this wedding and all its hoopla because you're sure everyone is going to think you're all sad and pining away over the groom?

Well, now this little turn of events changes that. Problem solved. Poof."

Kit put her hands over her eyes. "I can't believe you're encouraging me to perpetuate this lie. It'll never work."

"Look at me." Rylee pulled at one of Kit's hands. "Look at it as a misconception that just so happens to be a gift dropped right into your lap. When the wedding's over, you can say you broke up with the guy. You said he's only going to be at your place for a few months. It's perfect. Genius, even."

"A perfect disaster, more like."

"Maybe, maybe not."

"Kitty-Cat, look," Co-Co's voice came from outside the room. "I'm ready."

Kit groaned and went to the doorway. Co-Co stood on a pedestal in front of a full-length mirror. Gram's gown clung to her frame with Aunt Dee Dee again pinching the excess in her fist from behind. Under the overhead light, Kit saw that the fabric was still in such good shape, and the passage of time's pearly tone made it all the more beautiful. A tear pricked at her eye, but she was quick to blink it away. What hurt most was that she knew damned well Co-Co didn't go for things like this. She liked shiny and new. Co-Co went for bling. This dress situation was just more of the little snake's upstaging.

"Well?" Co-Co turned away from the mirror and tilted her head as she fixed her gaze on Kit. "Say something."

It was a long moment before she could formulate any words. She had to admit Co-Co's figure did Gram's gown justice. But her cousin was an imposter in the heirloom, and that's what fit her best. Kit took a deep breath; she couldn't believe she was really going to do this. But it seemed like the only right thing in this wrong moment.

"Let's get this done," she said. "I've got a boyfriend to get home to."

It was interesting how at this moment the big fat lie tasted better than a boatload of ice cream.

Chapter Eight

Alone with him in her house, standing there in her living room, Kit decided Shane Dugan filled the space. Her insides twisted. There was nowhere to turn. She squared her shoulders and made a split-second decision there was no way in hell she could live under the same roof as this too-cute fireman. She had to undo this nightmare right here and now.

Ever since Brian and his lip-lock with her stupid cousin, she was closed to the idea of a man, any man whatsoever, zooming around in her orbit. It made life easier that way or at least somewhat sane. In the time since she and Brian had broken up, she hadn't had an iota of interest in men, hadn't noticed anything about a single one of the species who crossed her path. Now Shane Dugan was here in front of her, pale-blue shirt draping his broad shoulders, clinging down over his taut torso, and disappearing into a tuck of his faded jeans that fit like custom. Oh lordy, no way.

"Thanks for agreeing to let me rent your room." His smile was dazzling. "I know you were hesitant about it at first, but I promise most of the time you won't even know I'm around."

She looked away, and her gaze landed on his T-shirt logo, *Sycamore River Fire Academy.* "Actually…" She hated this part, but this was a no go.

"And," he said, all smiley. He pointed a finger in

the air. "I'm handy. I can fix things."

"I, uh, don't have anything that's, um, broken." *Except my common sense. Yeah, that's worse than my Honda that got carted away in pieces.*

"But if you ever do, I'm your man."

No, Shane Dugan. Do not tell me you are my man. Trying to cut down, thanks.

"I appreciate that, Shane, really, but..."

"And don't worry about that cousin of yours. I've got no problem letting her think I'm your boyfriend for a little while." He placed his large, manly hands on his chest, fingers splayed. "Like that would be a tough job for any guy."

Parts of her that had been on ice were coming alive, her resolve melting in a succession of drips of maybe and puddling at her feet. What the heck was going on? No good would come from this thawing he produced.

"I don't know." She uttered a little laugh. "In hindsight I'm thinking I should just pull the plug on this now. It's too crazy."

"Crazier than that cousin of yours stealing your boyfriend and then expecting you to just be okay with it? Now that's crazy."

After all this time why did it still feel good to have someone else put voice to the injustice she'd had to deal with? She was over it. Well, she was over Brian, anyway. Last time she'd seen him, all she could think about was how big his Adam's apple was and how it looked as if he'd swallowed a hamster or something.

"Yeah, that was pretty shitty. But so is lying about having a boyfriend. It's just not me."

He blew out a big breath. "Okay, look, I agree it's

kind of out there." He laughed that nice sound while his eyes sparkled at her. "And it's your call, but like I said, I've got no problem playing along."

She turned away, and folding her arms across her chest, she paced around the sofa. "What about your girlfriend?"

"Dana's not coming home until Labor Day, and when she hears the circumstances, she won't mind."

"You're going to tell her about this?"

Shane shrugged. "I was going to wait until she got home, but yeah."

Kit continued to pace. "We don't know anything about each other. How are we supposed to pull off being in a relationship? It'll be like living with a pop quiz hanging over our heads all the time."

"Hey, I'm a quick study. Ask Hop. He'll tell you. We'll go over some basic stuff to make it sound legit."

"By Saturday?" She stopped her pacing and stared at him. "My aunt is hosting a dinner party on Saturday, and my mother is coming home from her cruise in time for it. Oh my God. My mother will be there. She's a bloodhound."

"First off, thank you for not doing laps around the couch anymore because it was making me dizzy." He tilted his head, as if waiting for her to smile, which she did, and his famous grin broke out across his mouth. "Good. Maybe you're starting to see the humor in the situation. It'll be okay."

"You haven't met my mother."

"By Saturday we'll be so convincing even your mother will believe it's true."

Could they really do this? The ruse had to be better than telling Co-Co and her mother that what they saw in

Rosie's Bridals was a façade for their benefit. Her humiliation was already at full tilt.

"And with regard to the, uh, PDAs, I think we can dial that back." She tried to cast the soft touch of his lips at her temple from her mind and the way his strong arm felt around her shoulders.

"Oh, you mean the smooch?" He pointed to his own temple. "If you want us to look like a real couple, we're going to have to act like it."

"Okay, but no lips."

He saluted her. "Got it. Lips are off limits."

She was doing this. This cute guy was going to move into her house and act to all the world like he was her boyfriend. There really was no turning back.

"Then I guess we forge ahead."

"Great."

"So, okay, let me show you around." She watched his eyes scanning the room, and she assessed the place as if she were seeing it for the first time.

The double windows in the front of the room covered by wooden blinds looked frilly to her now topped with that pinstriped valance and the pom-pom trim. The oatmeal-toned, loose-pillow sofa with the gingham-plaid pillows seemed sort of fussy. The butler's tray coffee table appeared too petite, like doll furniture. Was the rattan side chair strong enough to hold a hulky guy like him?

"Really nice." He returned his gaze to meet hers. "Cozy."

His eyes intrigued her with their springtime tones, and his lush eyelashes served as a canopy over them. Somewhere inside she thumped, and she turned away abruptly. "The, uh, kitchen is this way." He followed her through a doorway.

This small square room was her favorite. She loved her kitchen with its stubby little free-standing island crafted of butcher block darkened with age and the wood surface rutted from the years of use. Her old enamel stove with the squeaky door worked great, and she'd keep the relic until it bit the dust. She even appreciated the retro yellow Formica countertops and the white-painted cabinets with their black wrought-iron hinges with points like arrowheads. It was home.

"Cute," Shane said. He knocked his knuckles onto the butcher-block surface of the island. "This is nice."

"I should tell you now I'm kind of a neat freak." She watched for a reaction. If he was a slob or anything, she was screwed. "I like order."

"I can appreciate that."

"And you can use the kitchen, but you'll need to clean up after yourself. No dishes in the sink or anything."

"Got it. I don't really cook unless you count English-muffin pizzas." He laughed. "I mostly do take-out, especially now that Dana's in Milan. It's a six-month stint, and she's more than two months in. It's for work. She makes perfume."

She looked away from him. Something in his voice sounded wistful or kind of sad. Noticing stuff like that would be a no-no going forward. She would not get too friendly with this temporary renter. She'd gotten pretty good at keeping her distance from men and needed to continue to hone that skill.

He pulled a check out of his back pocket and handed it to her. "I'm going to need a written note from you for the fire department stating I lease a room here.

This is three months' rent in full, like we discussed at Hop's."

She took the check from his hand. "When, uh, were you planning on moving in?"

He shrugged. "I can move in whenever you're ready. My stuff's all packed."

Kit folded the check. "Want to see the loft?"

"Yes," he said. He followed her across the room, and then he took the steps behind her.

With each step she wondered what her butt looked like and cursed again the snacking habit she'd adopted since The Incident.

At the top Shane glanced around the loft, taking in the space. "This is plenty of room." He walked across the flooring. "Nice hardwood."

She pointed to the banister that looked out onto the vaulted living room. "I figure we could put some blankets or something over this to give you more privacy." She pointed to the door across the space. "And there's a bathroom in there."

"I'll be sure to leave the bathroom tidy, too. Like a Boy Scout."

She laughed. There was something so charming about this fireman and definitely not in a Boy Scout kind of way. She tried to shake it off. Her immunity already showed signs of wear, and she needed to repair it like a busted seam. She'd keep the fact he had a girlfriend in the forefront of her mind like a talisman, wear that fact around her neck like a necklace of garlic, and she'd consider Shane Dugan a vampire. Yup, that was how she'd do it.

Chapter Nine

By Saturday morning Shane had all his necessary stuff loaded into the back of his truck, and his furniture and the plastic buckets stuffed with nonessentials were in storage. He was ready.

He'd tried connecting with Dana twice, and both times she wasn't around. The time difference was a problem, sure, but something niggled at his brain. Over the last few weeks their conversations had become hurried, superficial, or wound up with a terse ending.

Maybe he was just thinking too much, but he couldn't help it. Their lives were on opposite ends of the world in more ways than geography. He looked over at his laptop that sat on the passenger seat next to him like a companion. Tonight in his new digs, he would try to reach her again.

He drove down the gravel driveway to the salt-box-style house with the nut-brown, weathered siding that would be his home for the next three months. Grateful for the opportunity, he had to admit the circumstances of living here were more than unusual. But he didn't have a problem acting like they were boyfriend and girlfriend. If he were honest, Kit Baxter was one of those girls he'd have gone for in a big way if they'd met in another time and place. Although Dana was a blonde, and he liked blondes, he really had a thing for brunettes. Kit's hair was long and sleek. She could rock one of those shampoo commercials. The shiny, deep brown strands swished around her shoulders when she moved her head. His fingers itched to just reach out and touch it.

That made matters tricky. He wasn't a two-timer, never had been, and he wasn't about to cross any lines now. But, man, she was appealing. Hey, he was human. He was glad his captain, Hop, was her friend and neighbor and he'd invited him to come by some nights to watch a ballgame. Between that and hanging at the firehouse, he'd put space between himself and his new landlord with the eyes like Bambi and the swingy, dark hair.

But so what if she was good looking and that in front of her ridiculous cousin, they'd have to play pretend. He smiled, remembering her adamancy of no more lips to the side of her head or any other place on her body. Her vibe was as clear as if she had secured herself behind an electronic fence. Keeping that in mind, he relaxed. He wasn't about to get himself zapped.

As Kit directed, he went over to Hop's house to pick up his key. He knocked on the front door, and Hop immediately opened it, big smile on his face.

"There he is," Hop said as he swung the door wide. "My new neighbor. Welcome to the river."

"Thank you. It's going to spoil me living here on the waterfront knowing I'm headed for the high-rise apartment building on the Green."

"I bet." Hop pulled the house key from his shirt pocket. "And whatever you do, don't lose this thing." He placed the key in Shane's palm. "She'll have your head." He chuckled, and his eyes were filled with affection for Kit. "Want to sit a minute?"

"Can't now, Hop. I've got to unload my stuff."

"Want a hand?"

He didn't want to impose on the guy, but somehow Shane thought he'd insult him if he didn't accept his offer. "Sure thing."

Together the two men unpacked Shane's vehicle. They carried the boxes, shirts on hangers, shopping bags of his shoes, towels, and other things. Together they maneuvered his mattress and box spring up to the loft.

When they were finally done, Shane saw that it was already five o'clock. Kit would be home soon. *Home.* Home with Kit Baxter. Trepidation trickled down his spine, like a bead of sweat.

"Want to go get a beer, Hop? I'm buying."

"Ah, next time, Irish. I'm doing the late shift tonight, and I've got to get ready." He gave Shane a light punch in the shoulder. "Keep your nose clean for these next three months so she doesn't kick you to the curb. That girl's no nonsense."

Shane laughed. "I'll keep that in mind."

He was tempted to tell Hop about their other arrangement, but he figured if Kit wanted Hop to know, she could tell him herself. He was pretty sure acting like a couple in front of her family wasn't something she'd be broadcasting around.

"You got everything?" Hop asked as he went through the front door.

"Just have to get my laptop from my truck."

Shane followed Hop across the driveway. He opened the passenger door, pulled his laptop into his grasp, and tucked it under his arm. He checked his watch. "I think I'll give Dana a try." He tapped the laptop with his other hand. "She's been hard to reach these last few days."

"Uh-huh."

"What do you mean *uh-huh*?"

Hop lifted one shoulder, then let it fall. He shook his head. "You ever get tired of that computer being your girlfriend?"

"It's only temporary."

Hop walked toward his own house before he turned back to Shane. "You young kids today crack me up. I like my women where I can touch them."

A silver car pulled into the driveway, and Kit got out of the passenger side. She bid the woman driver goodbye, and slowly the car backed out. Hop had made it as far as his front stoop but didn't go into the house. Shane focused his gaze on Kit as she strode across the gravel. She looked pretty today in a navy-and-white, pinstriped, summery dress and sandals that tied at her ankles. Her hair shone with a million facets in the late afternoon sunlight. What was she thinking with her mouth pressed into that straight seam? Her chest rose and fell in a deep inhale.

"Hi." Her voice was low. She uttered a nervous-sounding laugh.

"Hi."

"So this is it."

"Moving day." He punctuated the words with a nod.

Without moving her head, she shifted her eyes in the direction of Hop's house. "He's watching, isn't he?"

He couldn't help it. He laughed. The quirky relationship between his captain and his new landlord was interesting, and they weren't fooling him with their snarky banter.

She rolled her eyes and looked in Hop's direction. "Are you just going to stand there?"

"Hello to you too," he said. He angled a thumb in Shane's direction. "He's all moved in. Between the two of us, it took no time."

****

She pinned on a smile, but it felt tight on her face. Right now she wanted to turn around, dash to her room, and lock the door. But she managed a nod, offered a lackluster "great."

"Well, I've got to run."

When Hop started to turn toward his door, her heart fell. Suddenly being alone with this virtual stranger was impossible to deal with.

"Want to come over for dinner later, Hop?"

"Can't. I'm working tonight."

"Oh, okay." She made sure her face did not show the disappointment. After Hop waved and went in through his screen door, she turned back to Shane, and her insides clenched.

What was she doing? How had this become her new normal? She stole a glance of her tenant, then quickly looked away. What was going on behind his compelling eyes? Oh God. Those eyes and the cute fireman they belonged to would be living in her house. She hadn't thought this through by any means. How would they do the day-to-day? The nighttime hours?

"Well." A sheepish smile only made his face more appealing.

She repeated the word. "Well."

But neither of them moved an iota. They stood

there in the driveway. With Hop gone into his house, they were alone to let their new status sink in like water to soil. They were instant roommates, a couple playing pretend, and two pieces to someone else's puzzle.

Chapter Ten

Inside her cottage the walls felt as if they were closing in. This was going to be a long three months.

Shane gave her a sheepish grin. "You feeling as awkward as I am?"

"Yup."

"How's Romano's pizza?"

"The best."

"They make a grandma pie?"

"Yes. It's, uh, my favorite."

"Okay, to celebrate moving-in day, let me get us a pizza." He pulled his phone from his jeans pocket and tapped his fingers on the screen. She wished she had something to do with her hands, too.

"Um." She didn't want to start this arrangement off by doing dinners together. She wanted to draw a line between them from the get-go.

He looked up from his screen. "What toppings do you like?"

"What?"

"Pepperoni? Peppers and onions?"

"Oh," she said. "Um, plain."

He tapped his screen some more, then slipped the phone into his back pocket. "They should be here in twenty minutes. I put some beer in the fridge. Hope that's okay."

She looked at the refrigerator as if she'd never seen

it before. "Sure."

"Want one?"

He walked past her and went into the kitchen as if he lived here. *Oh God.* Not even an hour in and she was so filled with regret she might explode. She followed him into the kitchen, like a guest. He pulled a beer from the fridge shelf and looked up at her.

"I don't really like beer." She stepped around him and peered into the cavern of the appliance. He had taken over a full shelf with his food supplies, all crowded in a haphazard fashion.

"I, uh, see you've added some other items in here."

"Yeah," he said as he twisted off the cap of his beer. "That okay?"

She turned to face him. "Can I ask you why you have four bottles of ranch dressing?"

He gave her a grin. "You know how it is. You go in the food store, and you can't remember if you have dressing at home, so you buy another one."

"That doesn't happen if you keep a list. I make lists."

"Uh-huh."

She reached for the half-empty bottle of white zinfandel.

"Ah," he said. "Pink wine."

"It's not pink."

He snapped his fingers. "Right. You don't like pink."

Well, he retains information. That would be good for when they needed to recall details about each other for the big fat lie they were involved in.

He took a swig of his beer, and she couldn't help lingering her gaze on the strong muscles of his neck, his thick forearm as he held the bottle up to his mouth, the bulge of his triceps. When had she formulated an addendum in her resolve to hate men? Apparently, now she'd decided she could notice them.

Kit went to the cabinet, withdrew a wineglass, and poured herself a measure. They needed to come up with some rules about space. She could not spend the next three months in the same spot in this house with this appealing fireman. She tried to have her mind chant that he had a girlfriend, as she'd promised herself she'd do. But it didn't want to.

He was looking at her in a way that threatened to turn her inside out, and she quickly lowered her head to study the fascinating floor tiles. "I don't mean to be difficult. About the, um, stuff in the fridge."

"You're not. Hey, this is your place, and all of a sudden you've got company. I get it."

She lifted her gaze to meet his and could not look away. Her ridiculous insides did a shimmy. She sipped her wine.

"Um, you have any paper plates?"

"Yes." She went to a cabinet and opened the door. "And I'll get some napkins. And we'll need the pizza cutter," she said without looking away from her task.

"I'm pretty sure pizza comes already sliced up."

She flashed him a look. "I know that. But sometimes I like to cut a slice in half."

Shane shrugged, and she ignored the look on his face. "Okay. Where is it?"

She pointed without looking. "In that drawer."

He went to the drawer and slowly and respectfully pulled it open.

She watched him peruse the contents of the drawer.

Everything was lined up in perfect order the way she liked it, but right now her fastidiousness seemed silly.

"Wow," he mumbled under his breath. "This could be a surgeon's tray of kitchen gadgets."

"It's just more efficient, that's all."

Shane tilted his head and chuckled. "Measuring spoons in size order. Knives with all handles facing the same way, twisty ties in a little cup." He withdrew the pizza cutter and held it up to her. "Efficient."

"Are you picking on my junk drawer?"

"That's a junk drawer?" He laughed.

She cracked a smile. "I like order."

"So I see."

The doorbell sounded, and he went to retrieve their order from Romano's. A couple of minutes later, he came back into the kitchen with a boisterous announcement of "Dinnertime!"

He put the box onto the kitchen table and flipped open the lid. Half the pizza was plain, and the other half was covered in slimy-looking, wilted green peppers and translucent strips of onions, too reminiscent of the fateful chili dog she'd wolfed and then tossed into a trash can.

"Bleh," she said.

"Oh, come on." He lifted a slice into his hands.

Her fingers curled at her sides. Did this guy believe in using utensils, or did he have to just touch everything?

He nudged a slice with his fingertip. Did he plan to manhandle the entire pie? Her stomach flopped. What was next? Would he start licking all the slices?

"You don't like peppers and onions?"

"Not on pizza."

"Try it."

She handed him a paper plate. *Please don't stand there eating over the box.* "No, thanks."

She picked a plain slice he hadn't yet touched and slipped it onto a plate sans spatula. *When in Rome.* But she didn't take a bite of the pizza. Instead, she took a nice big gulp of her white zinfandel.

"Okay," he said after a swallow. "So Saturday is our first time to show your family how we're a couple. Am I right? Isn't that what I heard your cousin Cokie say?"

"Her name's Co-Co, short for Cordelia."

He shook his head. "How are you even talking to her?"

Kit snickered. "I have to tolerate her. In my family we all make nice-nice. My mother and her sister, Co-Co's mom, are so close, and I don't want to be the cause of any divisiveness between them. So for my mother's sake, I'm keeping the peace. Just getting through it." She couldn't believe how pathetic she sounded saying it out loud. "I realize it sounds lame."

"Okay, here's what we do, then. We do our very best to be convincing so you get through the wedding festivities." Shane looked at his watch. "And I'm supposed to FaceTime with Dana in a few minutes. I'll tell her the story so it'll be all on the up and up. She'll be fine."

"Oh lordy, what are you going to say to her?"

He shrugged. "Just the simple truth. One hand washing the other. I'm pretty sure she'll be cool about it."

"This is a disaster."

Shane tossed another piece of pizza crust on his

paper plate. He wiped his mouth and hands with a napkin. "It's not like we're doing anything wrong. I'm just helping in a tricky situation. If I tell Dana the circumstances, she'll understand."

Suddenly she wondered why he was so sure his girlfriend wouldn't be bothered by his pretending to be involved with her. Would he tell this girlfriend there was nothing to be worried about because Kit was so undesirable? Why was she feeling off-put by this? What did she care? She was losing her mind.

Her cell phone sounded, and when she slipped it from her pocket, she groaned. "My mother," she said to the ceiling.

"Game time." He pushed up from the chair. "I'm going to make that call to Dana."

Kit put her phone to her ear and with her other hand opened the refrigerator door. She pulled the wine bottle out by its neck.

Regina Baxter didn't wait for a greeting but instead charged right in. "Kitrina, I'm going to pull your hair."

"Nice, Ma. Good to hear from you."

"Why do I have to hear big news about my only daughter from my sister? What's the matter with you? I'm your mother. You only get one mother, Kitrina. You have news, I'm first. You don't hide things from me."

"Ma, listen…" Kit poured another glass of the wine. "You've been on a cruise." She took a sip. "So I wasn't going to call you ship-to-shore for the status of my dating life. And it's not that big a deal."

"No? What do you call living with a man?"

Kit plopped down onto the wooden chair. "Okay, yes, he moved in…"

"What's his name? My sister said he's a fireman, and she thinks he's Irish."

"His name is Shane Dugan, and it's true he's a fireman, and yes, I'm pretty sure he's Irish."

"You're pretty sure? How well do you know this man that's living with you? And is there a ring coming? No daughter of mine is just going to live with a man with no plan for the future."

She downed the rest of her wine. "He's nice. That's what I know about him, okay? He's nice."

"I guess we'll see for ourselves at Dee Dee's dinner party."

Kit considered switching to hard liquor. She was sure there was a bottle of some dark-brown, poison-tasting stuff in the cabinet leftover from Christmas. She was instantly reminded of the horror of this past holiday season when Co-Co and Brian discovered they were *meant to be.* She had bought the liquor to help drown the memory of it but hadn't been able to choke down more than a single sip of a substance that to her unsophisticated palate was no tastier than cough syrup.

Shane came back into the room and went into the fridge for another beer. She pointed to the phone at her ear and rolled her eyes. He offered a crooked grin.

"How'd you meet him anyway? Did you go online like I told you to do? My friend Mitzi met a millionaire on a dating site. They're very happy. He bought her a convertible, if you can stand it. I think I might try it."

"No, Ma. I, uh, didn't meet him online." She watched for Shane's reaction, expecting another of his pleasant smirky smiles, but he seemed distracted. He sat at the kitchen table, peeling the label off his beer bottle.

"How did you meet this fireman, then? Were you

on fire?"

She slid her gaze over to Shane. They'd have to come up with an ironclad story on how they met, and they needed some kind of cheat sheet or something with regard to personal details. This was going to be work, especially with her bloodhound of a mother.

This was the craziest thing she'd ever prepared to do. She didn't do crazy things. She was the sensible one, the reliable one, the good daughter, the kinder cousin. In one mad moment she'd shot all those attributes to kingdom come.

"I'll answer all your questions on Saturday, okay? But for now, I have to go."

"Okay, okay," her mother said. "I have so much to do anyway. I taped my soaps and have to catch up before I see your Aunt Dee Dee. She likes to ruin it for me if she's seen it before I do. And there's big doings on *The Bold and the Beautiful*."

"Mom, Mom...." When her mother went off on a soap opera tangent, it was tough reeling her in. One time she'd held up the line at the deli when she was talking soap opera with the lady slicing her no-salt turkey breast. "We'll catch up some more tomorrow, okay?"

"But you haven't told me about the car situation. I'm so sorry, sweetheart, that the debacle with the dead tree happened while I was away."

She filled her mother in on the tree and the car, leaving out the part where she had no money to rent a new vehicle, hence the new pretend boyfriend.

"And that awful man next door to you actually helped you get it all squared away?"

"Yes, Mother, and Hop's not awful. He's all bark

and no bite."

Her mother inhaled deeply through her nose. "I don't know why you befriended him."

As much as she loved her mother, Kit had to admit she tended to judge people by their covers. God love her, Mom's first meeting with Hop had been when Kit had first moved into the cottage. He'd stood outside with the moving van, giving orders to the two guys carrying her things into her new house. He'd just taken it upon himself to supervise the operation, which, in truth, had been pushy. All Kit had known at the time was her neighbor was an older man who went by the name of Hop. When Mom was moving too slowly across the driveway, carrying a punch bowl, a house-warming gift Kit knew she'd never use, the two movers couldn't get around her with her headboard. Hop had called out a "Move it, sister." That was all it had taken for Regina Baxter to dislike the guy. "Of all the nerve."

Mom switched gears. "I can't wait to meet your man." The words came out in a singsong that rose in pitch with each word. Ever since Mom noticed that Oprah, her idol, tended to talk like that when she was excited, she had adopted the habit. "I'm so happy for you." More singsong.

When the call was over, Kit turned to Shane. His green eyes lacked their usual glint, and they appeared darker, almost olive toned. Maybe he was realizing himself what a crazy prospect this was. Maybe his girlfriend wasn't as understanding about this lunacy as he had hoped. Maybe he was backing out, and then what would she do? She couldn't give him his money back even if she wanted to. She'd already put in the paperwork for a two-year lease of a sweet little Chevy.

There was no saying never mind to car dealers.

She had to find out what Shane was thinking. "Well, it's official," she said. "My mother can't wait to meet you."

"We'd better get our story straight then, huh?"

"Shane." His name felt foreign to her lips. "Did you Skype with Dana?"

"Yes, but just for a minute. She was in a hurry. Shocker."

She didn't know what he meant by the sarcasm, but a strange twist was going on in her stomach. Was Dana going to tell him to pull the plug on this lie?

"Did you talk with her about our, uh, arrangement?"

He held her gaze. "There wasn't time."

An awkward pause hung in the air, and after two glasses of wine, she felt a little fuzzy brained and unable to fill the void with any quips to coax that jovial expression back to Shane's face. She liked the easy smile he usually proffered. Instead, she just stared at him.

Finally, he locked gazes with her. "I think Dana might be seeing another guy."

Chapter Eleven

Shane didn't know why he'd blurted that out. At this point he didn't even know if it was true. Yeah, Dana had been acting aloof and seemed totally immersed in her dealings in Milan. That didn't prove she was cheating. He released a lungful of air. But that man's watch on the nightstand couldn't be explained away, and it was fishy that each nightstand had a glass of water on it. Dana's behavior was questionable as well. He wasn't a suspicious guy—it wasn't in his nature—but he wasn't a fool either. Her abruptness of late indicated something was up.

After he foolishly told Kit what he surmised, awkwardness filled the air between them. She had her own issues to worry about, and the last thing she needed was her new tenant to be unloading his girlfriend problem. It was an easy excuse to tell her he needed to tackle some of the stuff up in the loft, make the bed, all that. But that look on her face followed him up the stairs to his quarters.

Each time he looked her way, her Bambi eyes just stared at him, as if waiting for him to elaborate or maybe hoping he wouldn't. Either way, he couldn't get into it, and worse, he couldn't wrap his brain around the feelings that zipped around in his system. He was mad, yes, if it was true. Nobody liked being deceived. But what got him the most was the steady trickle of relief that dripped into his veins like water from a faucet that needed a washer. It surprised him. It bothered him.

Up in the loft he put on the overhead light and got to work. He assembled the bed frame and flipped the box spring in place, then positioned the mattress on top of it. He dug through some boxes, found the sheets, and finished the bed. He grabbed the bag of towels and went into the bathroom to take a shower, wash off this day, drown his thoughts.

****

Kit wrapped the leftover pizza in aluminum foil and put it in the fridge. She did some tidying up of the kitchen while her mind buzzed with thoughts of Shane. Despite her efforts to pull in enough air, her chest felt locked. She hadn't known the guy for long, had come into this whole disaster with a level of confidence he was completely untouchable.

A vision of his broad chest and muscular arms slithered like a thief into her mind. She'd thought about touching him, even let the fantasy play out in her head because it was safe and that zinfandel was messing with her.

She poured herself a glass of cold water and guzzled. Shane was taken. She was not like Co-Co. Kit didn't go near somebody else's man. It never occurred to her going into this that he could become single. She shook her head. Who said he was on the verge of that? He didn't. All he said was he thought maybe his girlfriend might be seeing someone else. Maybe it was just his loneliness for Dana that made him question her. Maybe it was baseless. And maybe it wasn't.

She put on the teakettle and made herself a cup of chamomile. It was eight o'clock, and the river called her. Everything felt better, easier, against the backdrop of the sounds of the water rushing by her cottage.

She brought her mug of tea out through the back door and walked across the small wooden platform that served as her deck. She eased herself into a wicker chair and leaned back. The evening breeze was welcome on her face and satisfying as it whipped through her hair. She sipped her tea and savored the warmth traveling through her.

But the host of issues came to her like bees that needed to be shooed. A niggle of apprehension crept into her system. She sipped her tea again. The time would come when she'd be through the wedding debacle and the whole sham she and Shane had agreed to pull on her family. Then it would be over. Her loft would be hers again. Shane would be gone, back with Dana, reconciled and happy, or not. It didn't matter to her. She would be free and unencumbered by budding thoughts she did not want or have the right to feel.

"Hey." Shane's voice startled her from her reverie.

She opened her eyes, and in the glow of her outdoor lamplight, his hair was shiny, slick, wet. He'd taken a shower, and the scent of soap wafted to her nostrils. He had changed clothes. He wore pull-on gym pants and a T-shirt with the name of a country band she knew and enjoyed emblazoned across the front.

"Hey." She put her mug down on the small glass table next to her. "Finished unpacking?"

"Almost. It's nice out here." He took a seat in the chair across from her. "I didn't want to invade your space, Kit, but today's Thursday, and it occurred to me that if we're going to pull this off with your family in just two days, I'm going to need some background. You up for that tonight?"

She sat up straight. He was right. They knew virtually nothing about each other. Yet tonight something happened—at least inside her it did. Nothing good would come from having a thought like that. She shook it. There was work to do.

"Okay, how should we start?" She placed her elbows on the chair arms and laced her fingers. She had the thought of asking him if he was okay with regard to his comment about Dana but dismissed it as none of her business. "I guess we should go over the basics."

He swept his fingers through his hair. "Why don't you fill me in a little on your childhood, your friends, college, postcollege, and your life since?"

She grabbed her mug from the small coffee table and took a sip of the tea, then cradled the mug between her hands. She told him about her family dynamic, how she and Co-Co grew up in the same town and went all through school together, how Co-Co had been a pain in the butt since day one. She told him a little about college and her love for needlework. That seemed to intrigue him.

"Did you always know you'd want to sew?"

She tilted her head. "Yes, but mostly I love beading. When I was a kid, I used to sew beads in patterns on my jeans and on my denim jacket. I'd make some of my own clothes, too, but the best part is always in the details."

Shane nodded. "Makes you happy."

"Yes."

"That's how I feel about being a fireman. It's something I've always wanted to do. Up when I lived in Roxbury, I was miserable working as a foreman in a warehouse. It paid really good money, and that was important. What made me happy, though, was being part of the volunteer fire department there."

"You like danger?"

He let out a little laugh. "I guess I must. I'm about to play a part at your family's dinner party on Saturday night. Seems pretty dangerous to me."

She laughed, too. "Yeah. Wait until you meet my mother. Be scared. Be very, very scared."

"Tell me how it went down with cousin Co-Co and your ex-boyfriend."

She groaned. "I'm so sick of thinking or talking about them, but for our purposes let me give you a brief synopsis." She told him about finding them under the mistletoe, how they professed their true love for each other amid their apologies.

"That had to be awful."

"It was. But now that some time has gone by, I have to say the worst part of it was having to admit I was so wrong about the guy. I really thought he could have been *the one*." She chuckled. "Stupid."

"It's not stupid to believe in someone you care about."

She pulled her mouth sideways. "Yeah, but the signs were there. I just wouldn't look at them."

Shane nodded and looked lost in thought for a second. "It can't be easy to have to face this whole wedding thing," he finally said.

She shrugged. "It's not great, but since it all went down, I've opened my eyes about Brian. And Co-Co, well, I guess she'll never change."

"Opened your eyes in what way? Realizing you two would have been wrong for each other?"

He sounded as if he spoke from experience, but she kept that thought to herself. "Brian and I didn't laugh. I mean, how could you spend your life with someone that doesn't make you laugh? And I don't know…If I ever decide I'm going to make somebody my partner in life, he's got to *get* me. Do you know what I mean?"

"I think I do."

"Full disclosure there, Fireman—and this will be good for you to know in case it comes up in conversation—I'm kind of a goofball nerd. I read old books, and old bookstores are better than a vacation to me, poetry makes me cry but in a good way, I love my houseplants, and yes, I talk to them. I paint my own nails and not pink." She flashed her navy-blue polish. "I like different. So I have learned one thing, and that's when *the one* comes along, he's got to appreciate that stuff about me."

"Brian didn't, huh?"

She thought about the time they were going out to dinner with his work friends. She'd fussed with herself that night, put on mascara, used a wrap instead of a sweater over her sleeveless dress. She remembered how he'd eyed her up and down and how she'd waited for his approval, like Oliver Twist wanting some gruel. Instead, though, he focused his gaze on her hands, her nails painted a cool-as-hell shade of turquoise. "What color would you say that was exactly?" The question had been posed not in fascination but rather disdain.

She shook the memory and looked over to Shane, who studied her. "No," she said with certainty. "No, he did not."

He nodded, a solemnity in his eyes.

Her insides squeezed. She cleared her throat and

regrouped. "Your turn. Tell me about you."

He told her about how he'd lost his mom and then his dad and how he'd become guardian to his younger brother, Nick. He told her about quitting college, his pride in his brother now that he was an accountant living up north with his wife. She learned how Hop and Shane's father had served in Vietnam and had been close through the years.

"Did you know Elinore?" she asked.

A smile broke across Shane's mouth. "Sure. She was a nice lady."

"He talks about her a lot. I can tell he really loved her."

"Talk about making each other laugh. They were quite the couple. She was scrappy. He liked that about her. Hop would dole out his best bull crap, and she'd call him on it every time. She had his number. I'll tell you that." Shane shook his head. "But yeah, they were something together."

"Hey, next time you're over there visiting Hop, look at the framed picture that's hanging up in the kitchen hallway of him in his yellow kayak. You'll see a look in his eye that sums it all up. That couple *got* each other."

"I'll do that."

"He must have been devastated when she died."

He held her gaze. "It was tough on him. She's been gone a long time, and as far as I know, Hop's never gotten involved with another woman."

"I'd guess it's because some things are so good there's no replacement." Kit pulled in a breath and exhaled. "Or finding another person that *gets* you in your lifetime just might be too much to ask."

They were quiet. No words came to her. What could that possibly be like—to have a relationship so wonderful that any other possibility paled?

She needed to fill the space. The nearness of him was too apparent, the topic too intimate. She pointed to his T-shirt. "You like country music."

He brightened. "I do. You?"

Their conversation continued into the night, covering topics that would become handy when they were at her aunt's dinner party on Saturday night. They shared favorites—favorite bands, favorite songs, and favorite ice cream—rocky road for him, almost any flavor for her, but there was nothing like a good vanilla.

"All the flavors in the world and you like vanilla the best?"

"Yes. But good vanilla. You know, the kind where you can see the little specs of vanilla bean in it."

"How do you know they're not bugs?"

She laughed. "I think I'd know a bug when I saw one in my ice cream. Oh, and sprinkles. Have to have sprinkles."

"Chocolate or rainbow?"

"That's a ridiculous question. Of course, rainbow."

They covered sports and movies, and she was amused at his surprise when she revealed her penchant for scary films.

"I don't think I've ever met a girl who likes scary movies. I mean, do you watch them through your fingers while you're covering your eyes with your hands?"

"No. I don't like blood-and-guts movies, though. I'm old school. *The Exorcist*, *Invasion of the Body Snatchers*."

"Black-and-white version or the remake?"

"Black-and-white."

He seemed to like that; the smile was back on his face. His eyes twinkled in the lamplight. "So you don't scare easy?"

She offered him a smile. "I'll let you know after Saturday night."

It was odd telling a virtual stranger about her life, but it was exhilarating, too. She liked the way Shane engaged, held his attention rapt. It felt good, as if a seed of friendship had been planted tonight.

Later in her room, she lay tucked under her hand-sewn summer quilt, the windows open and the breeze blowing through the screens and making the curtains dance. Her mind danced, too, with the new things she'd learned about Shane.

Not every guy would take on the responsibility of a younger brother, make the kid his priority. Not every guy would take on a job he detested because it kept the roof over his and his brother's heads. And the way his eyes lit up when he talked about the fire academy, the guys he was getting to know, how he liked Hop. She smiled in the darkness. They had that in common. They both liked Hop.

Above her head she heard Shane's footfalls on the hardwood in the loft. It was impossible to not picture him up there, maybe stripped down to boxers. She remembered what he said about Dana only because she had asked him outright. He'd told her he and Dana dated for about six months, and in the beginning their relationship was fun, exciting. She knew lots of people and lots of places to go, and it had felt like a whirlwind. The truth now, he'd said, was their long-range plans didn't seem to mesh. He'd shrugged, and she hadn't pressed him further. She hadn't wanted to know anything else about Dana.

Finally, thankfully, tiredness swept clear her crowded thoughts, and she fell asleep.

****

It had been a restless night, and this morning Shane ordered his coffee black at the local shop. He got a cup for Hop and drove over to the firehouse, where he knew the captain would be on duty.

Hop's office was on the third floor of the old brick building. On his way up the staircase, he stopped off on the second floor where a large, open, multipurpose space stood quiet now. The room was used for meetings and social gatherings, and just off the space was the big, industrial-looking kitchen where, according to Hop, magical meals happened.

He peeked into the kitchen. Two firemen were unloading groceries and supplies from cardboard boxes.

"Hey, NG."

Shane came closer. He didn't know these guys by name yet, but he'd seen them during a drill or some other activity. He didn't know how to respond because *N* and *G* were not his initials.

"Don't mind him," the other fireman said. He was a short, stocky man with spiky, black hair and a smirk of a smile. "Hi, I'm Larry. This is Dennis. In case you didn't know, *NG* stands for *new guy*."

"Oh." Shane laughed. "I get it."

"You here to see the captain?"

"Yes. Is he up in his office?"

The one named Larry nodded. "If you're still around at lunchtime, come have some lunch. We're making subs."

He thanked them for the invitation before he climbed up the flight of stairs to the third floor. Hop's office door was open, and Shane peered in. "Hey, Hop."

The captain looked up from his computer screen. "Good thing you showed up, Irish. I was about to throw this damn thing out the window."

Placing the two cardboard coffee cups on Hop's desk, he came around to look at what was going on with his computer. The system was performing an update.

"I have no patience for this stuff." Hop pointed to the coffee cups. "Which one is mine?"

Shane sat in a chair. He wasn't even sure why he was here, but somehow he wanted to see a friendly face. Last night had been interesting, and he'd found himself unable to get comfortable in his new space in the loft of Kit's house.

The time they spent together on the deck had given him insight on who this Kit woman was, what made her tick, where she came from, even if it was a study session so they could effectively pull the wool over her family's eyes on Saturday.

"What's on your mind, Irish?"

He shrugged. He didn't know where to begin. Did he want advice? Did he want to spill his guts on what he was about to portray with his new landlord? No. He'd promised he wouldn't tell anyone.

"Everything okay in your new digs?" Hop's brow pinched.

"Yes, sure, it's great. Kit wrote out a temporary lease agreement, and we're going to the bank and have it notarized. The arrangement's, uh, just what I needed.

Thank you for helping make this happen."

"Look, I brought you two together to solve each of your problems. Call me Mr. Fix-It." Hop pushed up from his chair. "I'm done with this stupid computer for today. Slow as molasses. How do you rely on one of these machines to keep you in touch with your girlfriend? That's got to drive you batty."

He blew out a breath he hadn't realized he'd been holding. "I'm starting to think maybe it is a lot to try and hold on to a connection when one person is here and the other is in Europe. But to tell you the truth, Hop, it could be more that's wrong with me and the girl."

"I'll tell you one thing, Irish. No job would have convinced me to move my ass clear across the world from my Ellie. And you know what? I'd swim the distance today if I thought she was there alive and waiting for me."

He'd known Hop loved his wife, but his open sentimentality surprised him. Being a widower for a long time, Hop obviously longed for the woman he'd lost.

Shane's heart tugged. Did love like that exist nowadays?

Maybe. It was hard to fathom when the woman he was supposed to be involved with became more and more distant as the days and weeks went by. And the evidence in her hotel room gave him reason to wonder if there was someone else.

If it were true, he wasn't sure how he even felt about that. His thoughts were a jumble. What did not help one bit was his agreeing to the deal he'd made with Kit. He was actually practicing how to be someone's pretend boyfriend. He was love's worst enemy.

"Come on, Irish. Let's go down to the kitchen and see what those guys are doing about lunch."

Chapter Twelve

Kit pulled Hop's uniform's double-breasted jacket from the back seat of her car. He had an important meeting coming up, and the brass buttons had needed securing, especially the ones that fastened over his belly. She'd keep that to herself.

She went in through the side door and took the steps to the second floor. Passing the kitchen, she paused in the doorway. Hop and Shane sat on tall wooden stools at the large worktable, and two other guys were with them. Each man chomped on a sandwich the size of a football.

"There she is." Hop wiped his hands on a napkin. "You hungry?"

She went into the room. A short guy with black hair gelled up in points picked up a brown paper bag. "We've got more rolls if you're interested in a sandwich. I make my own dressing."

"Thank you, but I'm good."

"I'm Larry. This is Dennis, and you know Hop, and this is—"

Shane stopped him. "Kit and I already know each other."

Larry's brows rose. "You do?"

"She's my landlord. Temporary landlord until my apartment's ready. Remember I was telling you about that?"

"Ah," Larry said. "Good to meet you. It's Kit?"

"Yes," she said. "Nice to see you guys. Hop, I've got your jacket ready." She lifted the garment covered in a plastic bag by the hook of the hanger. "Good as new."

"You're too good to me, kid."

"Don't I know it." She reached over and plucked a potato chip from his paper plate.

He playfully swatted at her hand. "Come on." He scrambled off the stool. "Go with me to my office. I want to talk with you about something."

She caught Shane's eye, and a rush of heat climbed her face. He had such expressive eyes, and it amazed her that after only knowing him for a short while, she was starting to read him. Right now he looked about as awkward as she felt.

"Bye, guys." Painting on a smile, she avoided looking at Shane.

****

Up in Hop's office, she sat in the guest chair. She snickered when he went around the side of his desk and gave his laptop a disgruntled shove.

"Hate that thing." He wrestled the suit jacket from the bag and slipped it off the hanger. He shrugged into it and buttoned the buttons.

"How do I look?"

"Like a movie star."

"I do, don't I?" He touched a finger to each button. "You did good, kid."

"I aim to please."

He took off the coat and put it back on its hanger, then hooked it over the top of his door. "Seriously, thank you."

"You're welcome."

"So how's it going with your new tenant?" He plopped down into his chair. "I can't tell you what a lifesaver you are for him. I know you did this for me, though, so I appreciate it."

She didn't like deceiving this man who tended to slay her dragons on a regular basis. She caught herself grimacing. "Hop, there's something I should tell you about that."

"Oh jeez. Already?"

"Hear me out, please, and don't lecture me either."

"This ought to be good." He clasped his hands behind his head. "Okay, lay it on me."

"First off, my mother's coming home from her cruise."

"Whoop-dee-do."

He liked her mother about as much as she liked him. Now was not the time to debate their mutual disdain.

"And as you know, my cousin is getting married soon."

"Yes, to the putz that used to be your boyfriend."

"And she's asked me to do the alterations of my grandmother's wedding gown for her."

"How nice of her. How about a pint of blood to go with it?"

She couldn't help it. Despite her nerves, she laughed, then quickly cleared her throat. "So here's what happened. Shane came to my job to talk with me about the possibility of moving in. My cousin was there with my aunt and the dress and overheard the conversation between Shane and me. They came to the wrong conclusion that he and I were moving in together because we are a couple." She used air quotes for that last word.

"Oh brother. This can't be good."

"Well, I made a split-second decision to let the two of them and eventually everyone else in my family think it's the truth. And, um, he agreed to go along with the phony story, and that's why I rented him the loft."

Hop scratched at his bald head. "You've got to be kidding me."

"I'm telling you this for two reasons. I'm not fond of fibbing to you, and in case you come in contact with my mom or anyone else in my family, I'm going to need you to play along."

He studied her face. "This could blow up in your face, kid. Are you aware of that?"

"It's only for a little while."

He shook his head. "A lot can happen in a little while. But I'll play your silly game." A smirk claimed his mouth. "Anything to show up that rotten cousin of yours."

She bit the inside of her mouth to banish the emotion that swelled in her. "Thanks, Hop."

"Hey, what's that old saying? 'All the world's a stage.' Right?" He scratched at his head again. "Let's hope it goes like you want it to."

Yes. Let's hope.

Chapter Thirteen

With their busy schedules, Kit and Shane's paths crisscrossed over the next two days. Relief washed over her when she'd come home and discover he wasn't there. His presence made her think until her head hurt. She focused on having to get through the dinner at Aunt Dee Dee's house. And in a blink, Saturday sneaked up on her like a thief.

A surreal calm blanketed her as she stared into her open closet. She perused the garments, the favorites she wore for fancier occasions. Since Christmas Eve's incident, sugar had been her drug of choice, and some of the dresses didn't fit her at the moment. But they would someday.

At the back of the closet were the impulse buys that had been one-hit wonders or hadn't even lost their tags. What had she been thinking buying floral palazzo pants? She shoved the hanger back even farther in the closet.

Her hand instinctively went to the navy shirtwaist, a comfortable, nice, and loose staple designed to hide a multitude of sins like paneling put up to remedy bumpy old walls. She stared at the garment. Would she ever break away from the nondescript? As she was about to unhook the hanger from the wooden dowel, her eye caught the tomato-red number all the way at the back of the row of dresses. She'd bought the dress on sale at the mall, had promised herself she would become the kind of person who was comfortable in a red, slim-fit dress.

She withdrew the sheath and before overthinking it, pulled down the zipper and slipped the dress over her head. The zipper resisted when she tugged it up, but all in all, somehow the dress fit, and mostly she was able to breathe in it. She slipped her feet into the nude-toned, heeled sandals and stepped in front of the full-length mirror behind her bedroom door. Not bad. She had to admit it. She took in views from each side. Did she want to make a statement like this when she arrived at the dinner party? Wouldn't it be better to blend into the woodwork, go unnoticed at her aunt's fussy soirée?

She tilted her head and studied the image in the glass. She decided she felt like Scarlett in her red dress when a widow's propriety called for head-to-toe black. Miss O'Hara hadn't wanted the label of being the woman left alone without a man. A thump of daring quickened her heart. Could she do it? Yup.

Shane waited for her in the living room. He stood by the fireplace, looking at the lineup of framed photographs on the mantel. Despite her resolve to stop noticing his appeal, Shane Dugan quickened her heartbeats. He wore black trousers and a pinstriped dress shirt open at the collar. He lifted his gaze to meet hers, and a grin broke across his face and traveled up to his eyes, making them sparkle like jewels. *Lordy.*

"You look nice." His gaze held hers.

She swallowed hard. "Back at you, Irish."

He pointed a thumb at the rest of the photos on display. "Are any of these memories something I should know about?"

"No, not for today anyway. Why? Are you getting

worried?" Panic was quick to pinch her gut.

He blew out a lungful of air. "I've never done anything like this."

"I know. Me neither."

"I'm kind of concerned about being separated from you and feeling cornered in a conversation." He uttered a nervous-sounding chuckle. "Maybe we should come up with a rescue phrase in case one of us gets stuck."

She mulled the suggestion. "That's a great idea. See, Fireman, you were born to rescue."

"It's got to be something that triggers us. Like an SOS."

"Okay," she said. "Let me think. An SOS."

He snapped his fingers. "I know. If I feel like a conversation is getting sticky, I'll say 'Hey, honey, let's share our surprise.' "

"Yeah, I get it, but then we need a surprise to share. We don't need to make things more complicated than they already are."

"How about we say 'Hey, what time is your appointment tomorrow?' "

"That could work," she said. "Let's just hope we won't need it."

****

They took Shane's truck for the drive to Aunt Dee Dee's. Kit was anxious to see her mother, who would be arriving by driver from the airport. Her stomach was like a blender whipping up a smoothie when she thought about her mom with her sharp eye and keen intuition.

As far as the other guests were concerned, Kit didn't know who else would be at the party, but she wasn't worried about fooling anyone as much as she was concerned about Mom. Aunt Dee Dee would be immersed in her hostess role, one she was born to perform, and Co-Co was notoriously so self-absorbed she wouldn't be a threat to their ruse. And Brian. *Lordy.* This would be the first time she'd be in the same room with him since The Incident. Oh, to blow off the event and go in search of a good chili dog.

"Okay." Shane cast her a glance. "One more time. Your middle name is Taylor, named after your paternal grandfather, you broke your arm in the fourth grade when you fell off the monkey bars, you never needed braces, your mom is Regina, and your aunt is Dee Dee, short for Deirdre. I know who Co-Co is, can't wait to see what this Brian looks like, and the rest of the people I'll just have to wing it as I go."

An easy chuckle escaped her lips. "You go to the head of the class. How about the story on how we met? Have we got that down?"

"Yes. We met at Jabberwocky's one night while you were waiting for your friend Rylee. I bought you a glass of chardonnay."

"Zinfandel, but yes, and I gave you my number, and our first date was dinner downtown at the Admiral Inn."

"I'm glad we kept it simple. I think we've got it, Kit."

She liked his smile and the way he said her name. As much as she'd promised herself not to keep noticing this fireman's appeal, nothing about her would cooperate. Her eyeballs liked the candy that he was. Her senses enjoyed his piney, manly man scent. She stole a glance as he kept his eyes on the road. Everyone would think she'd done well. A brick sat in her belly, though. This was not her man. She detested being a fraud.

"Turn here," she said as they approached Aunt Dee Dee's street. "And then it's the third house on the right."

"Wow. Lots of cars."

"Yes. And what timing." Her words escaped on a shaky breath. "That's my mother getting out of that gray sedan."

Shane shot her a smile. "You okay?"

"Hope so."

He flashed a reassuring grin. "We've got this."

"I'm glad you're so sure."

"Remember. SOS, if we need it."

He winked. She swallowed with a throat so parched it felt as if she were attempting to gulp down razor blades.

Chapter Fourteen

"My darling." Regina Baxter, arms spread wide, was flanked by a pearl-gray suitcase and matching carry-on at her feet. "Hello, hello," she chimed in that Oprah-style climb of intonation.

Kit and Shane walked together toward Mom, and with each step her heart gave a little pop, as if corn kernels were exploding in her chest.

Regina embraced her daughter, crushing her against an ample chest. "My baby," she said into Kit's hair. She pushed Kit away to give herself enough room to assess. "You look wonderful, baby. Healthy." She turned her attention to Shane, who stood by silently, his hands clasped behind his back. "Well, well," Mom said with an appreciative eye. "Hello there. You must be the new man."

"Hello, ma'am." He extended his hand. "I'm Shane."

Mom let go of her hold on Kit and pulled Shane into her arms. "Shane," she said over his shoulder. "It's a pleasure to meet you, young man. Oh, you smell good."

Jiffy Pop was going on inside Kit's chest with a steady stream of popping in her heart. *Lordy, Mom, let the poor guy go. And don't get too attached.*

Regina finally released him. She let her gaze flit between her daughter and the man beside her. "Oh, what a lovely couple you two make. And I can tell right away you are meant for each other." She clapped her hands. "What beautiful babies you'll make."

"Mom," Kit said through the clench of her jaw.

Regina waved her off. "Let your mother have some fun. You don't mind, do you, Shane? I'm just teasing you."

"Don't mind at all." He smiled. "Can I help you with your luggage?"

"Yes, that would be nice." Regina flashed an approving look at Kit. "Come on." Mom crooked her arm through Kit's. "Let's go join the party."

Together they navigated the cement steps to Aunt Dee Dee's front door. Shane followed with a piece of Mom's luggage in each hand. On the stoop Mom pressed her well-manicured finger on the doorbell. She gave it a series of taps. With each tap, another round of popping fired into Kit's chest, so much so her insides were running out of space for air.

Aunt Dee Dee greeted them first. Arms locked around each other, the two sisters laughed and rocked. The women were the same height, and it never ceased to amaze Kit how they tended to dress alike right down to the gold-tone, block-heeled sandals.

"You look fabulous, tan and rested," Dee Dee cooed to which Mom did a quick pirouette to give her sister a full-circle look.

"Notice how the gold-and-silver scarf complements my shoes? I bought it in Cozumel."

"Very chic." Dee Dee waved them inside with a hand. "Come in."

Shane placed the luggage in a corner of the foyer and came up beside Kit. She fiddled with the snap on her purse. Shouldn't they be holding hands or something? She didn't have the nerve to reach for his. She did, however, nudge herself a little closer so their arms nearly touched.

"Come here, you!" Dee Dee pulled Kit into her embrace, the funeral-floral scent twice as pungent today. She put her hands on Kit's cheeks. "Oh! You look so happy!" She reached a hand over to Shane, and he obligingly held it. "What a pleasure this is to see you."

Kit couldn't help it; an errant thought zipped into her, as if a bee had flown into her ear and was looking for a way out. Of course, Dee Dee would be happy to see her with a man at her side. He was the prop that would banish any leftover sourness on how the lovely bride-to-be and Brian came to be together. She closed her eyes and willed the thought away. Thanks to her new tenant, whatever this circumstance, she'd found a way to deal. She cast him a grateful look.

Dee Dee ushered them into the living room, which brimmed with guests. Some milled about, while others sat in covered folding chairs, the white fabric draped to the floor, and on the plush furniture. A portable bar was set up in the corner, manned by a tender in a white dress shirt and a black-satin vest.

"Get yourselves a drink and say hello to everyone." Dee Dee grabbed Regina, and the two sisters disappeared through the doorway to the dining room. "Dinner will be ready soon," she called back over her shoulder. "Co-Co and Brian are in the kitchen. Go say hi."

Kit pulled her gaze over to Shane. "Should we just get it over with?" she whispered.

"Want to get a glass of pink wine first?"

"I should get a shot of tequila, but yeah, I'll take some wine."

She accepted a glass of white zinfandel from the bartender, and Shane had a beer.

He tapped the bottle's neck against her glass. "Cheers," he said.

She took a good pull of the semisweet wine.

"Kit!"

She didn't have to look to know it was her cousin. Co-Co's voice pierced the air with a pitch high enough to bust an eardrum.

Co-Co stood with her arm crooked through Brian's. *Brian!* He stood there beside Co-Co with his new schoolboy haircut that accentuated the cowlick at the crown of his head, and he bore a sheepish expression so apparent it was as if someone had smashed a pie of contrition in his face. An awkward smile played over his lips, and it reminded Kit of two worms wrestling.

Co-Co, in a white-lace little shift that hugged her lean gym-rat lines and accentuated her well-toned arms, clapped her hands like a kid at a parade. Her hair was blown back over her crown, her makeup impeccably applied. Even Kit had to admit she looked stunning in a Barbie-gets-married kind of way.

Co-Co pulled Kit into a quick embrace and turned to Shane. "Welcome, Shane," she cooed. Co-Co cooed when she spoke to men, any man—the butcher, the baker, the candlestick maker. It didn't matter.

"Hi," he said. "Um, congratulations."

"This," she said with a voice brimming with pride, "is Brian."

"Shane Dugan."

The two men shook hands. Kit's gaze locked on the scene, as if it were a dream or perhaps a nightmare. She watched the two guys take each other in.

"Good to meet you," Brian said, then refocused his gaze. "Hi, Kit."

"Hello, Brian."

The four stood near the bar while people moved around them and chitchat buzzed in the air. They were a tableau of what had been and what was.

"How are things at Rosie's?" Brian asked finally.

"Busy," she lied. Falsehoods were her new way of life.

"You think you're busy?" Co-Co snorted. "I don't have a minute to breathe these days. Fittings, shopping, floral details, the music selections, the dance lessons."

"Dance lessons?"

Co-Co snuggled against Brian, and he slipped an arm around her in a possessive tuck. "Yes, Brian and I are taking dance lessons for the wedding so our first dance will be spectacular."

"And he's is on board for that?" She pulled her gaze over to him and tried to picture tall, lanky Brian and his size thirteen feet doing some fox-trot for the sake of a videographer. She didn't think he had it in him. However, the only thing she really knew for sure about him was that he was a douche.

"I got my shoes already," Co-Co stage-whispered. "I think I'll wear them to my first dance lesson. It's not bad luck for the groom to see me in my wedding shoes, is it?"

"Just don't sprain yourself doing the electric slide."

Hearing Shane's chuckle helped loosen the

constriction in her chest.

"Electric slide? You're silly. Anyway, Kitty-Cat, thank you for what you're doing for me with regard to my dress, which we will not discuss in front of you-know-who over here." She giggled. "Seriously, Kit, you're a lifesaver." Co-Co made a kissing sound that irritated Kit's ears. "You're too good to me."

No shit, Sherlock.

Aunt Dee Dee came into the room and announced dinner was served and everyone could come find their place cards, which was typically la-di-da of her. Kit watched Co-Co and Brian as they walked away and into the dining room.

While she and Shane went to find their seats, she did her best to banish thoughts about Co-Co and Gram's dress and her goddamn dance lessons with Brian. *Brian dancing.* That was priceless. Brain didn't dance. He tripped over those torpedo feet of his all the time. She tried to picture the two of them twirling around a dance floor and made herself dizzy.

She looked over at Shane, so handsome in his Sunday best, and her heart warmed at the good sportsmanship in this cute fireman. A thought flitted through her head again about Brian and Co-Co memorizing practiced dance steps that would take them in circles, leading nowhere. She was reminded of Shane's conversation about Dana, the way he confided in her about how he wondered whether or not they were going anywhere. As if he sensed her thoughts, he turned to her and winked. Her foolish heart giddyupped.

"Look at you two," Kit's mom said from her place at the table. Her eyes were bright with approval, and a nonsensical flush of gladness warmed Kit's cheeks.

She and Shane shared a look, and he reached for her hand. It was a gesture meant to fulfill their agreement, for sure. But Kit couldn't help noticing the warmth of his palm and the possessiveness of his touch. If she weren't careful, she'd fail to remember this was just an illusion.

Chapter Fifteen

Shane sat at the dining table with Kit at his right and Co-Co to his left. This little bride-to-be never shut up. She warbled like a bird on a branch.

He hadn't yet had the chance to talk with Kit again about his latest conversation with Dana and how she'd reacted to his and Kit's unusual arrangement. She hadn't liked the idea one bit and had called him a pushover. "You're always acting first and thinking later," she'd said.

The accusation hadn't been fair. He wasn't impulsive, not the way Dana was. He'd never contemplate living in another country just because someone made the offer, not without first considering the impact it would make.

After Kit had opened up about how she and Brian hadn't fit, he'd wanted to tell her what was going on inside him. Somehow he wanted her to know there was a crevasse in his relationship that had more to do with the people he and Dana were on a fundamental level than it had to do with their being on different continents or his agreement to play the part of Kit's boyfriend. But he hadn't had the chance, nor did he really think he could formulate the words.

He was glad he'd talked with Hop about it, although he didn't know what possessed him to open up to the captain the way he had. Hop wasn't surprised

Shane found Kit attractive, intriguing, fun to be around. Hop loved Kit. Shane hadn't missed the earnestness in Hop's tone in that subtle warning not to hurt her. She'd been hurt enough.

Beside him, Kit buttered her dinner roll. She cut the pat in half with the edge of her knife and spread the butter over the open roll. She paused, butter knife in hand, and then went back for the other half of the pat to finish the job. A smile fought to claim his mouth, but he managed to keep it in check when she looked up at him.

"Today carbs are my friend." She took a big bite of her roll, and as she chewed, a dab of butter clung to her upper lip.

"Any friend of yours." He reached for his own dinner roll.

She leaned in closer as she pushed the butter dish in his direction, and he inhaled her scent. She smelled like the honeysuckle that grew in a grouping near the riverbank outside the back deck.

"So far, so good," she whispered, her breath at his ear.

"No SOS necessary."

"Don't jinx us."

"So"—Co-Co leaned forward—"what are you two conspiring about?"

"We're discussing how good the rolls are." Kit took another big bite.

"Oh, Kitty-Cat. I envy the way you don't seem to worry about what you eat. I'm always counting every calorie." She patted her nearly concave midsection.

"Lucky for Kit, she doesn't have to," Shane interjected. He pinned on a smile, as if he'd won a round.

Co-Co shifted in her seat. "Let's hear how you two met."

Kit pointed to her mouth as her teeth worked over the bread. He flashed her a look she read loud and clear—*thanks a lot*.

"We met at Jabberwocky's," Shane said. "She was at the bar waiting for her friend, and I just couldn't resist going over to her."

Shane did not miss how Brian leaned in closer to listen.

"Tell me more," Co-Co cooed as she placed an elbow on the table and rested her chin in her hand. "Was it love at first sight?"

He looked over at Kit, who took another bite of her dinner roll. He knew what she was doing, and he couldn't help but chuckle. She was a cagey one.

"It was." He reached over and put an arm along the back of Kit's chair. "For me, anyway."

"How about it, Kit?" Co-Co leaned even more forward, almost putting her face on the table. "Was it like that for you, too?"

She flicked the tip of her tongue across the butter-slick pink cushion of her lower lip. She met his gaze and held it.

He bent forward to address Kit. "We just clicked."

Co-Co, seemingly satisfied, turned toward Brian, who was listening intently. Shane couldn't read his face, but unless he was having gastrointestinal distress, this conversation was making him uncomfortable.

"Like us, honey," Co-Co said in her syrupy tone. "Right, Brian?"

He cleared his throat. "Yes."

Shane didn't like this Brian guy. He didn't like his

looks or his demeanor. He seemed like a wimp, and what guy on the planet would do to Kit what he had done? Brian was a moron.

****

Throughout dinner Kit was amazed at how easily Shane talked with the guests. He complimented Aunt Dee Dee on the meal, although all she did was select menu items from the caterer. It was not the gratuitous chitchat that some people proffered. Everything Shane said appeared to be unplanned, genuine. She was in trouble. She was really starting to like him. Hard to believe a few months ago she'd declared men were more trouble than they were worth. That was before Shane Dugan showed up.

After dessert, guests milled about with after-dinner drinks. Some people wandered out onto the patio through the french doors off the living room. One of Dee Dee's nephews from Uncle Larry's side, Paul, had cornered Shane about his new hobby of fly-fishing, a sport Shane appeared to know a bit about. Paul's young daughter Abigail, Co-Co's junior bridesmaid, gazed up at Shane with a moony-eyed look of a girl with a crush. Kit's mouth curved upward.

Her gaze flitted to the doorway to the dining room, a view she couldn't avoid at this point in the evening after a couple of glasses of zinfandel. There was no sign of the hole in the molding where a pushpin had held the mistletoe in place in the center of the doorway. It must have been painted over, the smooth line of the wood like brand new.

She walked through the doorway and made her way to the big windows in the living room. She put her back to the view when it conjured the image of

Christmas Eve's dash over the icy driveway to get away from Brian and Co-Co.

A few steps away Shane was in conversation with Paul, making the guy laugh, which in turn made Shane laugh as well.

"Hi." Abigail did a pirouette in front of Kit. "Mama said she and Daddy are taking dance lessons. I take ballet."

"You're doing that turn very well, Abigail. Your lessons are paying off."

"I'm going to be a ballerina when I grow up. But I'm only nine now."

An arm wrapped around her shoulders. Mom. She gave Kit a kiss on her cheek, gave her a squeeze.

"Hi, Mom."

"Kitrina." Mom's voice was thick with emotion, making Kit turn to meet her eyes.

"What is it, Mom?"

"You." The crevices by her eyes were deep when she smiled. "I'm just happy to be here with you. I like your Shane."

A zing of guilt climbed Kit's spine like cold fingers tracing along each vertebra. But she managed a "thanks."

"Sweetie." Mom squeezed her again. "It's okay to feel nervous."

"Nervous? What are you talking about?"

Mom pointed to Kit's face. "Nobody knows you like your mama. Never forget that, girl of mine. I see the way you look at that man."

"Not sure I follow, Mom." She pulled her gaze away, looked down at her dress, and brushed off a nonexistent piece of lint.

"Come with me." Mom grabbed her hand. "Let's get away from big ears."

She dragged Kit away from the living room and ushered her down the hallway to the study.

The entire time Kit practiced the SOS signal. Would Shane hear it from the vantage point of Aunt Dee Dee's study?

In the square, paneled room, Mom pushed her down on the overstuffed loveseat. She took a seat beside her.

"Mom, this is silly. Why are we here?"

"To talk without my sister being Miss Nosy Pants." She leaned in close. "Ever since that whole mess with your cousin and Brian, things have been touchy."

Touchy. Kit smiled. That was one way to put it. With this family's habit of brushing their missteps under the proverbial carpet, the furniture should be tipped over from the uneven flooring.

"It's all behind us now, Mom. Co-Co and Brian are happy. I'm happy. Case closed."

"I'm glad, sweetie. That Brian wasn't for you anyway." She reached out and squeezed Kit's hand. "But I did catch that look you were giving Shane."

"What look?"

Mom shrugged one shoulder. In her sleeveless dress, her shoulder was tan and freckled from the sun. "Worried."

"Worried?" She scoffed. "Worried about what?" Did mother radar ever dry up or at least run low?

"Listen to me." Mom's eyes implored. "And listen good. I see there's real affection with you two. A mother knows. But I also sense your hesitation, almost like you're afraid to give in to it or like you think

113

meeting Shane was too good to be true. Don't think like that."

She opened her mouth to speak, and Mom hushed her by lifting her index finger. "Let me finish…" She settled on the seat and like royalty, crossed her legs at the ankle. "Do not let what happened with Brian taint your new relationship. Too many times we do that to ourselves, we women. We are always waiting for a shoe to drop. Don't. Enjoy it. There is no shoe that's going to fall from the sky and land on this new chapter of your life. Okay?"

Sadness or shame—Kit couldn't tell which—poured over her head like a bucket of paint, covering every inch of her, suffocating the fantasy she'd allowed herself just minutes ago. When her mother pulled her into a hug, she hugged her back harder. She felt sorry for her mother. The woman didn't even realize that she herself was the shoe that fell onto Kit's head and knocked much-needed sense back into her. Shane belonged to another. She'd almost forgotten.

"And, honey, you've been such a good sport about your grandmother's wedding gown. I'm hoping you've let go of the disappointment. It was just a dress."

"It was more than that, Mom."

Mom put a hand on top of Kit's and gave it a squeeze. "It marked one moment in your grandmother's life. You know that photo I found in a box in my mother's attic, the one with Gram on the steps?"

"Yes. You told me the dress was pink." She was tempted to make a face but didn't. Instead, she complimented what stood out to her in the picture. "It had a snazzy rhinestone belt buckle, right?"

"Yes, it did. Gram looked so happy in that

snapshot, didn't she?"

Kit nodded her head but didn't know what that had to do with Co-Co being the recipient of the wedding gown.

"Happiness is on the inside no matter what's on the outside."

When Kit went back to the party, guests were still lingering, some by a dessert table set up on Dee Dee's sideboard, some hanging by the bar. Shane stood with Brian, each of them nibbling on a cookie from the selections. Her insides did a tumble. As if reading her presence, Shane turned his head in her direction. The message in his green eyes flashed as though with intentional sequence—SOS.

Chapter Sixteen

Shane took another bite of the peanut butter cookie. How had he gotten roped into talking with this guy? One more word about the scuba lessons and the quest for becoming an instructor and he might toss his cookie.

"Enough about me." Brian took a bite of the brownie he had been nibbling like a rabbit. He closed his eyes and uttered a soft moan. "These things are addicting. So besides putting out fires, what do you do? What's your passion, Shane?"

"I have a lot of interests. Music is up there. I play guitar."

Brian nodded, unimpressed. "How's it going living on the river with Kit?"

"Great. She's got a sweet place."

"Yeah, guess you got pretty lucky, huh?"

He didn't like the tone of Brian's words, dripping with skepticism so profusely the guy might need a bib.

"Very lucky."

"Has she tried to convince you yet to get a pet?"

Shane swallowed hard. "Sure."

"I'm allergic so there was no way I was going to sleep over if she got one."

"I have no problem with dogs."

Brian tilted his head. "Cats. Kit loves cats."

"Right. That's what I meant."

"I'm sure you know all about Blue."

Blue? What did that mean? He was having brain freeze, as if he'd eaten too much ice cream too fast. Obviously, there was something significant about the color. Where was Kit anyway? He looked around for her, but she had disappeared somewhere with her mother a little while ago and hadn't returned.

"So?" Brian prompted with a quirked brow. "Did she?"

"We tend to have that in common, too. We, uh, both like blue."

"Blue was her gray cat that died before she moved into the house."

"Oh."

"How do you not know that? She was obsessed with that hairball."

Shane turned his head and thanked all the saints that Kit had come back to the living room. He met her gaze, willing her to come to the rescue. She picked up on his cue and closed the space between them with quick steps.

"What are you two chatting about?" She'd pinned on a bright smile, but Shane knew it as a facsimile.

It didn't matter. He was just glad she was there.

****

"Kit, how have you not told Shane about Blue? How long did you guys go out before you decided to move in together, anyway?"

Her mouth hurt from smiling, and she let it fall. Her face flooded with heated resentment. "Two months," she blurted, which came out the same exact time Shane offered, "Six weeks."

Brian was about to say something but stopped when Aunt Dee Dee sidled up beside them. She clapped her hands like a teacher wanting her pupils' attention. "Guests are beginning to leave, Brian. Come. Let's say our goodbyes. Your fiancée is by the door, waiting."

When Brian walked away with Dee Dee, Kit turned to Shane. Their eyes locked. They didn't need words. They both knew they'd dodged a bullet.

****

Co-Co and Brian stood by the front door, as if they were in a practice run of the wedding's receiving line, alongside Aunt Dee Dee and Cousin Paul, who would be walking the bride down the aisle as a kind of surrogate for Co-Co's father who'd passed away ten years ago.

Aunt Dee Dee pulled Kit into an embrace. "Thank you for coming." Her eyes were misted over.

Kit thought she detected a quiver in her aunt's artfully glossed mouth. Was this in an acknowledgment of what the lovely couple's circumstance had cost her?

She was tempted to respond with an "I wouldn't have missed it," but she was fresh out of fibs for today. Instead, she said, "You did a wonderful job, Auntie." The comment seemed to please her, and Kit couldn't decipher if the smile was in gratitude or relief. She worked her way toward the door, first with giving Co-Co a quick hug. "I'll see you for your next fitting in a few days."

"As soon as I lose the ten pounds this party put on me." She giggled at the absurdity of her words, and Kit was not about to tell the girl what she wanted to hear. Besides, she didn't have to.

"Koala-Bear, you hardly ate a thing," Brian chimed in. He squeezed her small waist. "I can ring one hand around you like a belt."

Koala-Bear? Kit swallowed the urge to laugh, but it was as if she'd swallowed a feather, and she started to giggle. She'd read somewhere that koala bears were cute, but in actuality they were pretty darn nasty. That sat well with her, the parallel satisfying and enough to quell her urge to laugh out loud.

When she stepped over to Brian to say goodbye, she saw from the corner of her eye that Aunt Dee Dee had Shane in her clutches, fawning over him. She cast him an I-owe-you look when their eyes met.

Kit gave Brian a perfunctory kiss on the cheek. "Good party." He had that wrinkle on his forehead he tended to get when he was contemplating or suffering from indigestion. He pulled her closer again, and for a breathless moment she thought he was going to kiss her on the mouth.

"Kit." His whisper was hot on her face.

She focused on an angry, red zit that had sprouted on his neck. She'd forgotten how he diligently fought the effects of oily skin.

"How well do you know this guy?" he asked.

"What?"

"Call it intuition, but I've got this feeling about him. I mean, I hope you haven't rushed into anything on a, you know, rebound or anything. I'd hate to think that's what this is."

Ire lit up inside her like a stick of dynamite with a fuse burning down rapidly and on the brink of explosion as each second being in his proximity ticked by. She took a step away. "Not your problem to worry about, Brian."

"Still care about you, that's all."

Throughout the ordeal that unfolded after The

Incident, she'd been playing nice in this imbalanced sandbox. She'd managed to keep her cool, show her teeth when she smiled, but right now she wanted to punch Brian in his sanctimonious face.

Thankfully, Shane came up to her and slung an arm around her shoulder. "Ready, babe?"

"Extremely."

****

Shane sat in his truck with Kit beside him as he drove back to her cottage on the river. Although it wasn't yet nine o'clock, the sky was black, and the inside of the truck glowed with the green lighting from the dashboard.

"Well, all in all, we did pretty well," she offered.

He flashed her a quick look. "Brian is suspicious."

She uttered a soft "I know."

"Let's just hope he doesn't share his suspicions with the rest of the family."

"Yeah."

"Other than that, though, I think we were a success. Right?"

"We sure fooled my mother."

"Really?"

"Oh yeah. That was why she dragged me away from the party to give me a talking to. Think witness stand in a court scene on TV."

His mouth curved into a smile. "Uh-oh. What did she say?"

"Well, let's see. She told me she can tell we are good together and warned me not to blow it by not giving in to my feelings."

She may have meant for her mother's interrogation to lighten the mood, but they both fell into an uncomfortable quiet. The cab of his truck closed in on him, stealing his air.

He kept his eyes on the road, gripped his hands hard on the wheel, and did his best to dispel the feelings that roiled in his gut. He wanted to turn his head again and look at Kit as she sat in the seat beside him. But he did not. He was, however, acutely aware of her. The honeysuckle scent that was either perfume or her shampoo teased his nose. He heard her breathing and the squeak of the leather seat under her when she moved. He couldn't take it. He reached over and turned on the radio.

A country tune came on. He couldn't remember the group that sang it, but he did know the song was about a guy in love. He switched it off. Talk. That was what they needed to fill in the space. He'd keep it casual and keep his mind from going to a place it had no right to travel.

"So..." He searched for words. "Your family seems nice." When she didn't immediately respond, he turned to look at her, and in the dimness of the truck all he could see were her eyes, big and dark, shiny. He turned back to the road.

"They sure liked you," she said finally.

"Did they?" He cast a teasing smile. This was good. Keeping it light. Friendly.

"Everyone said you were, uh, nice."

He let that sink in for a moment. Again, they were in an awkward silence. The silence fed the thoughts in his head, the stupid ones and the ones he could not cast away.

He exhaled a long breath. "And so that was Brian."

"Other than the third degree, what'd you think?"

He made a noise with his lips. "He's a putz."

Kit laughed and maneuvered her body a quarter turn to face him. "That's Hop's word."

"I know. The old guy's rubbing off on me. You seemed really surprised to hear about Brian and Co-Co taking dance lessons. Did that upset you?" From his peripheral vision he could see her fingers slide through the cascade of her long dark hair.

"Not upset. Surprised. Brian, or I should say the Brian I knew, would never in a million years take dancing lessons."

"No, huh?"

"Never."

"Did you hear that the whole bridal party is taking the lessons, too? And your aunt as well?"

"No," she said. "Where did you hear that?"

"I heard your aunt telling your mother. She even asked her if she'd like to take part. Watch out—they might hit us up for dance lessons, too."

He meant it as a joke, so her groan was a surprise. He pulled the truck into their driveway and slowly coasted down the gravel hill. He put the vehicle into park and unclipped his seatbelt. "Okay, so that hit a nerve."

Kit turned to him. "Add this to your list of what you need to know about me—I'm the world's worst, I mean worst, dancer. Just another reason to dread this wedding now that I know everyone there will have taken lessons."

"Maybe you're not as bad as you think."

"No, believe me, I am." She looked away from him, focused her eyes outside the windshield. "Brian once told me I was too uptight, said I was rigid.

Sometimes I think he was right. Maybe that's why I can't dance. It requires some form of abandon, I guess. I'm just no good at that."

Shane didn't know what to say about that. He wanted to tell her she wasn't as rigid as she thought she was, not based on the way she demonstrated love for her mother and even good old Hop next door. The way she laughed at Hop's corny jokes, the way she savored a perfect bite of pizza, a bit of buttered roll. And it was far from rigid being the bigger person around her cousin and that putz. He wanted to tell her that. But he wouldn't. Shouldn't.

"Tell me about Blue."

She leaned her elbow on the back of her seat, propped her head with her hand. "He was my cat. If we'd taken the time to go over those picture frames on the mantel, I'd have remembered to tell you about him. He was something special."

"How long did you have him?"

"Eight years. I got him as a rescue. He was part Siberian, which is a long-haired, big-bodied breed. He had this big fluffy tail that looked like a plume. Smartest cat ever."

"Yeah?"

"He played fetch with drinking straws."

"Really?"

"If I was in the bathroom getting ready for work in the morning, he'd shove a straw under the door for me to throw for him. So I'd open the door, toss the straw as far away as I could, and he'd go bounding after it. No easy task getting out of the house with Blue around."

"What happened to him?"

"Renal failure."

"You miss him."

"Down to my bones."

A hush fell over them, and they sat in the silence. Finally, Shane spoke.

"Let's go in."

Chapter Seventeen

The house was dark and still when they entered, and Kit darted across the wooden floor to flip on the kitchen light. In the golden hue Shane watched her with a new understanding. She felt it, too. He could tell. Something had switched in them tonight the same way the house had gone from dark to light with the touch of one finger.

"I, uh, think I'm going to place a FaceTime call to Dana," he said. Maybe he'd get lucky, and she'd be available. He'd decided, and he didn't know when he had actually formed the thought, that he was going to pin Dana down about their relationship. It wasn't just about the man's watch he had spied on her nightstand or her never being available. He had questions for her that went beyond those things. Was she happy? Was this relationship what they wanted it to be? He had those questions for himself as well. He also needed to tell her more about his living arrangement. Now that feelings were creeping in on the situation, telling Dana could not wait.

****

The call connected, and Dana's image appeared on the screen. She wore a white terry robe and her hair was up on her head in a sloppy bunch. Sans makeup, she was still pretty, and he'd never seen the need for her to apply such a ritual to her face each day. Yet she was in the beauty business, so maybe it was more of a need on her part.

"Hey, stranger," Shane said.

"Hi, Shane." Her smile did not meet her blue eyes. "How's it going?"

"I've been wanting to talk," he began.

"About?"

"Well, first off I wanted to tell you the story about my temporary-living situation."

"The apartment on the green with no balcony and no view. You told me."

"No, that's not until September. I needed to find housing from now until then. Remember? I told you."

She twisted her mouth. "Yes, of course. Okay. You've rented a room in Sycamore River until the apartment's ready. Sorry, my mind's all over the place these days. So how is it working out?"

Since it seemed as if she'd only half listened when he told her the first time, he reminded her how his coming to rent Kit's loft came to be. He told her how he had paid for the three months in advance. That set something off in her.

She moved her chair closer to her screen and pulled her lips in on themselves. "How much did you give her?"

"Two thousand dollars."

"Are you serious, Shane?"

She chastised him again about his impulsivity. She reiterated how she had tried telling him that joining the Sycamore River Fire Department and moving to the quiet community were rash decisions.

"You act first and think later all the time, Shane."

Granted, he hadn't really discussed becoming a

paid fireman with her, but he'd known how she'd react. And he'd been right. She went into her rationale again about wanting him to finish his degree.

"You only have a year left." Her tone was incredulous. "You could do most of that online these days."

"But then what, Dana? Get some office job and push paper around all day? It just isn't me. How can you not know that by now?"

Now it seemed silly he'd thought she would turn her feelings around once she came home and saw how happy he was to be a full-time fireman. Doubt grew stronger with each day. She was finding her Milan trip so successful and was all revved up about new possibilities. How would she ever be happy in a little town like this after getting an offer to live and work in Italy? Tonight reality stood in front of him like a roommate.

"Dana, when you get back, I think we need to have a conversation."

Her mouth twisted to the side. She unfastened her hair, and it cascaded down around her shoulders. She gave her head a shake. "No time like the present, Shane." She leaned in closer to the screen, her eyes imploring. "Say what you have to say."

He paused but shook his head. "Not now."

A blinking of light flashed under the closed door behind her. From past FaceTime sessions, he knew the door went to her bathroom.

"A light just went on in your bathroom."

"What?" She jerked herself around.

"Is someone in there?"

She faced the screen again. Her mouth opened,

then closed again. "Shane, I…"

"Look, Dana, be honest with me. I don't know who's in there or why. Right now, frankly, I don't really care. But shouldn't we just admit we're heading in different directions?"

She touched a finger to her lips. *"Frankly, you don't care?* Is that what you just said?"

He blew out a long breath. "You don't need to repeat my words back to me. If there's something going on with some other guy, I wish you'd have been straight with me about it. That's all."

She tilted her head and studied him. "You don't seem too bothered by the idea." Her gaze softened. "Living here in Milan, an offer to change companies, it's all so much. I think I'm conflicted."

No reply would have been productive. He had been feeling a disconnect with Dana for some time, and in just a few short days, he had been reevaluating everything. How much of that had to do with his brunette landlord, he couldn't even wrap his brain around. So in that respect, how could he be angry with Dana for having conflicted feelings?

"Let's do this." She cleared her throat. "Maybe we should just take this time apart to be on our own. You know, live our lives, and then when I'm back, we'll see where we are."

"I'm pretty sure I already see where we are."

"It's just that…"

"Dana, we don't need to rehash what's gotten us here." He shrugged. "Here we are."

She pulled her mouth in a downward curve. "Here we are."

****

After the call ended, Shane looked around his temporary home. The loft was arranged with an economy of his belongings, with most of his stuff piled up in boxes in the storage unit. A warm glow of light filtered up from the lower level. He heard Kit moving around down there and closed his eyes. Right now he needed to separate himself from all of this. The call with Dana had been disturbing yet resolute. He still needed to process what had transpired, and spending more time with Kit tonight would do him no good. He knew that much. He was already too mixed up.

He picked up his cell phone and found Larry's number in his contacts.

"Hey, Irish," Larry said when he answered the call.

"Hi, Larry. What are you up to?"

"Just got off my shift, so I stopped for a beer at Jabberwocky's."

"Want some company?"

"Sure, come on over."

****

Shane bolted down the stairs and announced he was going to meet a friend from the firehouse. Kit was relieved, really. She needed some space from the guy. Thinking about him was too confusing, and his presence was no help.

But she couldn't help looking out the kitchen window. She watched the red glow of his taillights as he drove up the driveway and made a left toward town. Her phone rang, the display telling her that it was Mom. She closed her eyes. Connecting the call, she opened the fridge and pulled out a new bottle of wine.

"Hi, Mom." She cradled the phone to her ear with her shoulder while she fiddled with the wine opener.

"Hi, baby," her mother singsonged. "Am I interrupting you two kids or anything?"

"What?" For a second she'd forgotten she was supposed to be one half of a couple. "Oh, no. Shane, uh, is meeting one of the guys from the firehouse."

"That's nice. I like when a man has friends, don't you?"

"I never thought about it, but yeah, I guess so." She pulled the cork out of the bottle and went to the cabinet for a glass.

"Believe me, Kit. You'll be glad he's got friends to go play with when you are an old married couple. It's good when they're not underfoot all the time."

"Mom, don't go jumping the gun, okay? Nobody said anything about getting married." She took a sip of her wine.

"Not yet, but I have a feeling…." Mom's voice rose with giddy anticipation.

After another sip, Kit asked, "Is there something specific you called about, Mom?"

"Yes, as a matter of fact. Did you know the whole bunch is going for dance lessons for the wedding?"

"I heard."

"Not just the bridal party, mind you. The whole family and some of their friends, too. Dee Dee wants me to take part. She even mentioned asking you and Shane."

"God, Mom, what's wrong with these people? Is this a Stepford wedding where everybody has to dance the same way or something?"

"Stepford? Who's that?"

"Never mind, but that's just ridiculous."

"I guess that means you two wouldn't be

interested."

"Hell no." She enjoyed another taste of her wine.

Mom chuckled. "Even if it means you can watch Brian attempt to be Fred Astaire?" Now she laughed out loud. "Can you imagine? That Ichabod Crane of a man trying to finesse those shovels he calls feet?"

Mother and daughter shared a laugh. Maybe it was the wine, but Kit got a kick out of the image her mother conjured by likening her ex to Irving's character from "Sleepy Hollow."

When the call ended, Kit's mood was light, and after a second pour of white zinfandel, she went into the living room and turned on the TV. Pushing buttons on the new smart device, she found what she was looking for. An instructional YouTube video on ballroom dancing.

Chapter Eighteen

Jabberwocky's was jammed when Shane got there, but he found Larry at the far end of the bar, nursing a pilsner of suds.

"Irish." Larry motioned his head to the empty stool beside him. "Take a load off."

He took a seat and waited for the bartender to come over. His head was spinning, and it felt good to be out. His conversation with Dana was on his brain as was the problem of his pull toward Kit.

"I know a man that needs a beer when I see one." Larry waved over the bartender and with a hand gesture signaled ordering Shane a drink.

He liked Larry. He'd been the one to take Shane under his wing with the other guys at the station. It turned out Larry was the jokester in the bunch. He was quick-witted and could spew out a caustic barb as if he had them waiting on the back of his tongue.

"So what's on your mind, my man? I could tell you've got some serious stuff to work out based on the way you took it out on that equipment you washed yesterday." Larry chuckled as he brought his glass to his lips.

"What are you talking about?" He thought of how yesterday morning he and Larry had detailed the hook and ladder. He'd been nervous about going to Kit's family party but mostly conflicted about Kit herself.

"You took it out on the equipment. Damn, I practically sat back and just let you go. Made my life easier, so I'm not complaining. Those trucks never looked so good."

Now Shane laughed. "Hey, maybe I was just trying to pick up your slack."

"Buddy, I figured it was some kind of therapy. Honestly, though, something eating you?"

"It's a long story."

"You worried about the certification test?"

"Who wouldn't be? There's a lot to learn, but no."

"Okay, that leaves the obvious. It's a woman."

Shane guzzled his beer, then looked over at his friend. "Try two women."

"Oh, okay, now we're talking. Irish, I'm all ears."

It felt good to spill his guts to a friend. He told Larry about his relationship with Dana and about her current gig in Milan. He explained how things were different with them and how each day it seemed as if they were more and more disconnected. He told him about their last conversation and how they'd agreed to take a break.

"Sounds to me like this chick's looking to have her cake and eat it, too, bro. She's over there in Italy and doesn't want to feel like she's messing around behind your back, so she's calling for some time off. You willing to wait around for her to come back and pick things up again with you?"

Shane shook his head. "I'm pretty sure that's not going to happen."

"That's one woman. What's the deal with the other one?"

Then he told him about Kit and his living

arrangement with her.

"Wait, so you're living with one girl and might be still dating another one?"

"No." His protest was loud. "Technically, maybe, but it's not like that. Kit, she's the one I'm renting the room from, was supposed to just be my landlord."

"But…"

"But, well, it's so complicated now."

"All ears, Irish."

So Shane told him about the way he'd needed a place to stay to meet the stipulations of the job. He told him about the ruse he and Kit were playing for the sake of her family, and as he reiterated the story, he could barely believe his own ridiculousness.

Larry laughed like hell. "Are you serious?" He laughed again. "It's like you agreed to all the bullshit of a relationship with none of the perks. Good job, Irish."

"This is just between us, Larry, okay? As it is, I feel like shit most of the time."

"Hope you're not feeling bad for the one across the pond. She's over there having some Italian fun. Why shouldn't you have some of your own?"

"It's not like that. I mean, honestly, I'm not sure there's any hope for Dana and me."

"Dana's the girlfriend."

"Yes."

"So? No problem, then. Is there something already going on with the landlord?"

"No." Shane finished his beer. "Up until now there was Dana, and I'm no cheater. But I don't know. Things are different now."

"I'm telling you, man, chicks complicate everything."

With a commiserating nod of his head, he patted Larry on the back. "I have to go, but thanks for listening."

"Hey, there are worse things to worry about than having two women in your life."

"Yeah," Shane said. He pinned on a smile he did not feel and tried to come up with something light to kill the dour mood. Larry was a fun guy, a quick friend, and Shane didn't want to have one of his coworkers thinking he was a downer or a pansy but a guy's guy. Early impressions mattered. "Two's tough. I better take my vitamins, I guess, huh?"

Larry emitted a crack of laughter and saluted his dwindling ale. "Cry me a river, bro."

****

On the way back to the cottage, Shane turned on the radio to drown his thoughts. His conversation with Larry replayed in his head, the sound of Larry's laugh at Shane's stupid comment about needing to take vitamins. Where had that come from? He didn't feel at all jovial or snarky about Dana or his growing attraction to Kit.

He reached over to find his favorite country station and was glad it was playing one of those shit-kicking songs with a lot of twang and steel pedal guitar. He was no singer—that was for sure—but he belted out the lyrics in the solitude of his truck, hoping the words would crowd out the troubling thoughts in his head.

He parked his truck and went up to the door of the cottage. The lights were on in the kitchen and the living room. Hand on the doorknob, he still felt odd to just walk right in. But he did.

He took in the scene in front of him in the living

room. With a half-empty wineglass dangling precariously in one hand, Kit faced a video playing on her flat-screen television. It was some sort of a dance tutorial with an old-fashioned looking couple, the blonde in a puffy pink dress and her hair up in a fancy sweep of stiff cotton candy, the guy mustachioed and wearing a tuxedo.

The man spoke to Kit from the screen. He had an accent, European of some kind, Latin. "Now, again," he said as he stared out from the television. "One, two, slide, together."

Shane watched as she attempted to follow along. The couple moved in unison with measured steps. Their eyes appeared glazed over, the woman looking off to the left, the man looking off to the right. Kit lifted her arms and held them in the air, as if she were with a partner. She stepped and stepped again. She slid her foot outward and snapped it back, tilting her body in the effort where she knocked against the sharp edge of the coffee table. An expletive shot from her mouth. He couldn't help it. He laughed.

At that she spun around and stared at him. She sucked in her breath, and a hand went to her chest, as if he'd caught her naked.

****

"When did you get back?" Kit spread her arms wide, a futile attempt to shield Shane from seeing the video. She wanted to shut the damn thing off, but the remote was on the sofa, and her feet wouldn't move. "How long have you been standing there?"

"I just got here."

"Well, you should have announced yourself or something." She willed her feet to carry her across the room to grab the remote. Behind her the man in the video called out "Let's try again, shall we?" She groaned. "You can't be sneaking up on me."

"I didn't," he said. "I mean, I'm sorry if I interrupted your, um, lesson."

She flew to the sofa and grabbed the remote. "Lesson," she said as she fiddled with the buttons. "Who said I was taking a lesson? I was just..." She thought she'd pressed the Off button but instead hit Pause. The man in the tuxedo and the woman he held in his arms were frozen in a stalled twirl, and the looks on their faces were ghostly with dull-eyed stares.

She turned from the screen and looked at Shane. Although his face was appealing with that smirky smile, she was tempted to throw the damn remote right at it.

He took a step closer and pointed to the screen. "Is, um, that an attempt to be ready for the wedding?"

"No." She took a swallow of her wine, eyes still on him. "Maybe."

"Kit, not for anything, but do you really think that's the kind of dance lessons the bride and groom and who knows who else are taking?"

"I don't know. I told you I know zero about dancing."

"Look at those two." He closed the space between them. "That guy there looks like the Count from *Sesame Street*, and that lady looks like she's from the fifties."

"Well, the video said it was *classic* ballroom dance. Who cares how long ago it was filmed? Classic is classic."

He took the remote from her hand. His fingers

touched hers, and the touch lingered for a moment while their eyes met. "May I?"

She finished her wine and put the empty glass onto the coffee table. "Okay, Fireman, let's see you do any better."

He pressed the button, and the outdated couple on the screen resumed their synchronized circling of the dance floor.

"Look at them, Kit. Do they look like they're enjoying themselves?"

Head tilted, she studied the screen. "Not really, but whoever said dancing was fun?"

"It is fun, though. But you'd never know it watching these people. Why would anybody want to move like them?"

Kit shrugged. "My entire family wants to, apparently."

"What do you want, Kit?"

She met his gaze. "Among all the other reasons to detest this wedding, I'd like to not be a loser wallflower while everyone else is doing that." She circled her hand in the air toward the TV screen. "As it is, I'm attending the event with my pretend boyfriend. The pretend boyfriend that everybody thinks is just wonderful, the one that makes my mother all twinkly eyed when she looks at us. The only thing I'm good at, apparently, is lying."

He laughed. "So your family's convinced we're a couple. Isn't that what we set out to do?"

"Well, yes."

"Okay, one problem down. Now, what's your biggest issue with dancing?"

"No rhythm."

"No rhythm."

"Zilch."

"You like music?"

"Yes."

"Okay, that's a start." He pushed some buttons on the device in his hand. "Let's find something from this century and see what happens."

"Shane, it's no use. I can't."

"Let's have a go at it."

She grabbed her empty wineglass. "I need wine."

In the kitchen she poured herself a half glass of the white zinfandel from the fridge. She took tentative steps to watch Shane as he scrolled through music videos on her television. His black hair curled at his collar, and she wondered what it would feel like in her fingers. *Stop.* She groaned.

Shane turned to the sound. "Hey, I found a good one. Come here."

Just the way he beckoned caused her insides to melt like chocolate on a stove. If she were at all wise, she would listen to that little voice in her head and go lock herself in her room. But she and her glass of wine went to him. Just moments ago she couldn't get her damn feet to move. Now, apparently, they wanted to dance.

A picture of a pop artist appeared on the screen while his song played. It was a more current song with an easy, pleasant beat, one that Kit recognized.

"You like this one?"

She nodded.

"Okay, so let yourself go with it."

"Go with it." She snorted. "Yeah, okay."

Slowly he began to step left and then right, his hips

swaying in with each step. It was an easy pendulum of movement. She swallowed hard.

She took a pull of her wine. *No way.*

"Come on. Just feel the beat."

Don't coax me to feel, Fireman.

She put the glass on the coffee table. *No more wine.* As it was, his swaying hips were making her dizzy.

He grabbed her hand and pulled her toward him.

"No, no, no…"

"Relax, girl. Here, stand in front of me, and I'll guide you." He turned her to face away from him. She felt his breath on her neck.

"I can't." *Are you nuts?*

"I'm telling you, Kit, give it a chance. Feel it, and then we'll take some steps. Okay? Move with me."

Feel it? Trying really hard not to, but yes.

Shane put his hands at her waist. An electrical charge ignited through her as if she'd been struck by lightning. She sucked in her breath, and he loosened his grip. She turned her head around to face him. The look in his eyes made her insides tumble over on themselves. Her heart thumped with the knowledge that this guy who was helping her with her ridiculous ruse was just trying to help her some more.

What the hell? She turned to face him and placed her hands over his. "Okay, Fireman, show me."

They swayed to the tune that floated from the speakers. They moved in unison, side to side, each step causing their bodies to touch. Maybe it was the wine, maybe it was the gentle and rhythmic touch of his body, his hands firm at her waist, but she felt herself softening, becoming malleable, liquid almost. She flowed on the tune that filled her ears. He spun her around slowly, and when she came around to face him again, his eyes held hers. She closed her eyes as the music enveloped her, entered her through each and every pore.

"You're doing it," he whispered in a low, soft tone as his face came close to her ear. "I knew you could if you gave yourself the chance."

She lifted her head to his gaze, and his hands did not let go of their hold. She and Shane continued their united movement, left and right with tiny steps, matching sways. His eyes shone bright with pride or some emotion that touched her. A kiss beckoned, and his mouth was perilously close.

Stop. This good and nice man belonged to someone named Dana. Kit halted her steps, and he almost fell toward her in her abruptness. If she didn't stop now, she would be no better than her selfish cousin. She was not Co-Co. She would not tread where she didn't belong even when every cell of her body wanted to.

"You okay?" His eyes implored.

"Shane, I, uh, appreciate your help—"

"You're dancing, Kit." His mouth curled into a broad smile.

"Am I?"

"Are you kidding me? Yes. You're doing it."

She laughed. The moment belonged to him, though. He led, she followed. And the song had ended.

"Thank you for giving me the lesson. You're better than that video I was watching."

"The key was going with it. Let the music be the guide."

She swallowed hard. "Well, I appreciate it."

"You're welcome."

His eyes held hers, and her heart stuttered in her chest. He was so close all she'd have to do was lean into him, and she wanted to. With every cell in her being, she wanted to.

"We can't do this." Her words were a whisper, riding out on a shaky breath.

Shane didn't respond, but his gaze remained locked on hers.

"We'd regret it," she continued to herself more than to him. "We can't hurt someone else."

"Dana and I agreed to end things."

Her heart fell from her chest. "You did?"

"It wasn't working."

"Oh."

"The truth is that things were off for a long time. She and I don't want the same things. Honestly, I'm sure she's relieved. She and I didn't work. But it was more than that for me."

Kit didn't know what to think. Her mind was a jumble of thoughts. Shane had ended his relationship. The truth was that she was developing feelings for him. Somewhere along the line the pretense they were playing had given her real feelings. Were they falling for their own ruse? His gaze searched hers. This was crazy. If she took one step toward him, she'd lose what little perspective she had at the moment. There would be no turning back. Her feelings were too new, and she was too raw.

"I should call it a night, Shane."

"Okay." He let his arms fall to his sides, and she immediately missed his touch. "Same here." He picked up the remote and switched off the television.

"Thank you again, though, for the dance lesson."

He smiled. "I knew you could do it."

"That makes one of us."

"Good night, Kit."

"Good night, Shane."

Kit went into the kitchen to turn off the light and make sure the back door was locked. She heard his footfalls up the stairs to the loft. With each step that carried him away, her mind implored her to call out. But she would not.

She padded down the hallway to her room and closed the door behind her. She stripped out of her clothing and pulled on an oversized T-shirt. She went into the bathroom to perform her normal nightly routine while trying to shut off her mind. She could hear the shower turning on upstairs, and her mind teased her with what Shane would look like naked under its spray.

Her chest heaved as thoughts circled around in her mind and whipped through her veins. Maybe it was the white zinfandel, but she could not erase that fireman from her mind, could not dispel the lingering heat from his touch on her skin.

She crawled in under the covers of her bed and pulled them up to her chin. Shane and Dana were over. Was it really true? When it came to men, she was terrible in discerning truth, yet from what she knew of Shane Dugan, he was no liar. The only lie the guy was guilty of was the one she'd convinced him to be part of.

She heard the water shut off upstairs. The creaking of the floorboards sounded in her ears. She tried to envision him as he walked across his room. Was his mind doing the same things to him? Was he thinking about her, too? Exhausted from her overactive brain, she finally fell asleep.

An hour or so later, she woke with a start. She thought she'd heard a noise downstairs and strained to listen, but the house was silent.

Needing a glass of water, she slipped out from her covers, and her feet found the terrycloth slippers. She crossed the room and slowly opened her bedroom door, doing her best to not make a sound. She made her way down the hallway to the kitchen. The moonlight filtering in through the window over the sink served as her beacon as she gently opened a cabinet and soundlessly withdrew a water glass.

"Hi."

Her insides squeezed as she turned in the semidarkness.

Shane.

Chapter Nineteen

"What are you doing up?"

"Couldn't sleep." Shane took a step in her direction. Moonlight cut across his face and illuminated his eyes. They were tender yet imploring orbs fixed on her.

"I was, um, getting water." Air suffered to escape her lungs. The empty glass sat in her palm. She gripped it.

"Kit…"

The way he said her name was like a plea, and her heart squeezed in response. Her feet carried her a breath closer. She put the glass down on the counter. The click of glass meeting the laminate surface was the only sound in the darkened room.

"Dancing, uh, isn't the only thing I'm bad at, Shane. My heart does some misstepping of its own."

"I know you've been hurt, Kit." He closed the space between them. He reached for her hand in the darkness and brought it to his chest. He pressed it. "I wouldn't."

She lifted her face toward his, and her lips parted naturally. Her heart stammered as her mind buzzed with all the reasons this was a bad idea. But those thoughts disappeared in the hammering of her heartbeats. Was she making one more bad choice? Just this once she was going to trust her feelings. Just this once.

Shane turned her hand over and brought it to his lips. He pressed a soft kiss to her palm, making the skin there tingle. And as if music had been turned on, giving her a reason to move, she pressed to him.

He claimed her mouth in a kiss, and heart thundering, she returned it. Her hands moved to bury themselves in his hair. Enjoying the thickness of the strands, she wrapped her fingers around them and tugged. A low moan sounded in the back of his throat as he circled his arms around her and squeezed her closer. In return she cradled his head and deepened their kiss.

He lifted her into his arms, and she wrapped her legs around him. Their bodies bumped in the doorway to the living room in a hasty move to the sofa, and together they collapsed on the cushions. A rush of greedy hands pulled and pushed at their clothing until their garments were tossed to the floor.

****

Shane pushed himself up and cast his gaze over Kit's naked form. She was beautiful. Simply beautiful, soft, and female. The tip of his index finger touched tentatively at her shoulder, and the sound of her sucking in her breath stirred him deep in his belly. Even in the darkness he could see her smoky eyes, moist with wanting, were locked on his. He ran that finger down a slow path along her soft, smooth skin. The pad of his finger was alive as it traced her contours, marking a path where his mouth needed to go. He ached for her.

As though reading his mind, Kit reached up and pulled his head down to kiss him again. The cavern of her mouth welcomed him as she deepened their kiss. His lips slid to her neck, the tip of his tongue tasting her salty sweetness. He pressed his mouth to her shoulder and languidly traveled his lips down her form, pausing to suckle and knead, searing a path to her apex.

Her soft moan nearly sent him over the edge. He buried himself inside her, and she lifted her hips to him. They moved together, a perfect rhythm in their fiery, intimate dance until their passion claimed them.

Chapter Twenty

In the morning Kit headed over to Rosie's Bridals for her fitting appointments with two brides-to-be, one of whom being her blasted cousin. But today even Co-Co didn't rattle her. She had bigger things to digest.

She was grateful Shane had already left when she'd gone into the kitchen after getting ready for work. The memory of last night punctuated every second she'd spent in her morning routine. Stepping down the hallway, she held her breath until she knew he had left for work already.

She was unsettled, off kilter. Despite the too-hot shower this morning, last night was alive in her mind and on her skin. Every time she closed her eyes, she saw his eyes and the hunger in them as he looked at her. She was a dichotomy of wanting to remember every nuance of their lovemaking and wishing she had an ice pick to stab into her frontal lobe. Instead, she ate a doughnut from the wax paper bag Shane had left on the kitchen counter. She saw the note and stopped midchew.

Good Morning

Had a feeling you'd be second-guessing last night. I hope you aren't. I'm not.

They didn't have any jellies left, so I got you a glazed.

Enjoy!

She stared at the message he'd written on a sticky note from the pad she kept by the landline. His printing was spiky and appeared hurried. She reread the words. She had to like a guy who knew she preferred a jelly doughnut over a glazed. Despite the admonishments that threatened her thoughts and sought to devour logic in gulps, her mouth curved into a smile. She bit into the doughnut and savored the sweetness.

As soon as she came into the workroom at Rosie's Bridals, she knew Rylee's antenna was up. Kit had never been able to hide much from her best friend. Besides, she was pretty sure she was beaming like a certified idiot.

"Good morning. You look funny. Everything okay?"

"Sure." Kit swallowed. The word had come out too quickly and too loud. Although she'd become an aficionado in the art of lying, she just couldn't fib her way around the fact that she was slightly nuts about a guy she'd only known for a blip of time. *Nuts* was indeed the operative word.

Rylee put down the paperwork she had in her hand and came over to where Kit stood at the rack of dresses that were awaiting alterations. "Okay, you want to fill me in? Something's up."

A million excuses pelted her brain, but she knew eventually she'd confide in her friend. Maybe Rylee would have some advice on how not to be a screwball over what happened last night.

"My first bride is due in about a half hour. Then I expect Co-Co around noon."

Rylee nodded as if she understood, but she didn't. This was not about Co-Co.

"Ry, I may have made the biggest mistake of my life last night."

"You didn't actually go over to your cousin's and chop off her bangs while she slept, did you?"

It was Rylee's attempt to lighten the mood. And yes, she had said she'd *like* to hack up Co-Co's perfect bob, but they both knew she'd never do such a thing. Last night, though, was up there on her list of shockers.

"I had sex with the fireman."

Rylee just stared at her. She blinked and blinked again.

"Yup. You heard me. I did him. On my couch. Twice."

"Oh boy. Um. Okay, then." Rylee put a finger to her lips. "And how are you feeling about that?"

"Hell if I know." She sat on one of the stools. "I was perfectly fine staying away from him despite his cuteness. You have to admit the guy's pretty cute."

Rylee's head moved in a slow, tentative nod.

"Despite his appeal, staying away from him was pretty easy considering he had the girlfriend over in Milan. Right? You know me better than anyone. I'm not a cheat. I don't cheat. But then he and the girlfriend called it quits."

"They did?"

"Yup. Done."

"How long ago?"

"Oh, like maybe five minutes." She put her hands in her hair and gave the strands a good shake. "At least that's what it seems like in retrospect. What's wrong with me?"

Rylee plunked herself on the stool next to Kit and touched her knee. "Look at me, Kit."

She lifted her gaze. "I'm insane."

"You like the guy, my friend. Even I've known that for a while. So I don't think you're insane. Preemptive, maybe."

Kit groaned.

Rylee rose from the stool and marched over to the minifridge. She withdrew a bottle of vitamin water and handed it to Kit. "Here."

"I need more than this if I'm going to drown myself." She unscrewed the top of the bottle and took a swig. "This should be vodka."

"How do you think he's feeling this morning?"

"He bought me a doughnut." She met Rylee's gaze. "Don't look at me all googly eyed. It could have been glaze-dipped repentance on his part. I mean, he just broke it off with the girlfriend. Who knows? Maybe they're already back together by now. And once again I've picked Mr. Wrong."

"I don't think he's Mr. Wrong at all, Kit."

"You don't?"

"I do not. Not the way he looks at you and the way he comes by the shop to bring you a coffee in the middle of the day, the way you light up when you talk about him. I think you two were destined for this to happen."

"Oh, Rylee, please don't go there with me. I might start to believe it. And I can't set myself up for more heartache. I can't be thinking this fireman is my Mr. Right."

"Okay, so give yourself a break then, Kit. Think of him as Mr. Maybe. How about that? Shane Dugan is Mr. Maybe."

She mulled the words. "Mr. Maybe."

Could he be? Could this really be the start of something real and good? She dared to allow one word to rest in her heart. *Maybe*.

Chapter Twenty-One

Shane finished early at the academy and itched to talk to Kit. He just wanted to hear her voice. But he refrained from contacting her. He knew what he was dealing with. Her breakup with Brian was months ago, but now with her cousin marrying the guy, the relationship-gone-wrong was in her face day in and day out. He blew out a lungful of air. Timing wasn't his strong suit.

But last night was something. His mind played it over and over again, the way she looked at him, the way her mouth fell open slightly when he touched her skin, her lower lip glistening, wanting him. He stirred. Man, he had it bad.

He didn't know what this meant, though. Was that a momentary lapse in judgment? Couldn't be. Kit wasn't that kind of woman. She didn't give herself on a whim. He must matter. But maybe not.

He got into his truck and sat there with his hands on the wheel. Was it bad news that she hadn't called him yet today? What did he expect? Had she found the note he'd left her? His mind was a roller coaster gone off the track.

After starting the engine, he turned in the direction of the firehouse and hoped Hop was there.

****

Co-Co arrived right on time, and this time she was

alone. No offense to Aunt Dee Dee, but Kit was in no mood to deal with the two of them today.

"Helloooo."

"Hi, Co-Co." Kit retrieved the dress from its plastic bag with a heavy tug of the zipper. The fabric was weighty to her touch, like the regret that had started to blanket her heart. She'd tried to hold on to the heady feelings of this morning, the delicious memory making her blush in the daylight. But as the minutes ticked by, doubt was a needle and thread stitching her uncertainty to her heart like a patch over a jagged tear.

She placed what used to be Gram's dress onto the hook above the dressing room door. After first-round alterations, the gown looked so tiny in order to fit her cousin's slight frame, almost like a costume for a preteen.

"Isn't it lovely, Kitty-Cat?"

"It is."

Co-Co pouted her lips. "So why aren't you gushing over it? You're the one who worked your magic." She touched the beading. "Look how beautiful. No one would ever know you had to replace the missing beads. Seriously, Kitty-Cat, you're a genius."

She didn't want Co-Co's accolades, given with the same conviction as anything she cast her approval upon. Wedding dresses and a bowl of salad greens got the same enthusiasm. In her world everything was *so beautiful.* She swallowed hard. For once in this crazy prewedding ordeal, her raw nerves had nothing to do with Co-Co.

"Did you take a grumpy pill today?"

"Not at all." Kit forced herself to end it there. What good would it do to sully one of the happy bride-to-be's moments? "I'm awkward with compliments, Co-Co. You know that."

Her cousin smiled something close to genuine. "Don't I know it."

Kit slipped the dress from the satin hanger. "Let's see how it looks, shall we?"

Co-Co clapped her hands, as if it were snack time in kindergarten, and traipsed into the dressing room.

****

"How's it going at the academy, Irish?"

Hop sat at his desk in the captain's office on the third floor, the two big front windows of the small room open and the blinds pulled up. Outside, downtown Sycamore River was alive and bustling.

"It never gets old. You'll see."

"What doesn't?"

"The way this town just gets in your blood. I look out this window each day and fall in love all over again. Like loving a good woman."

When he didn't comment, Hop narrowed his gaze, his furry eyebrows tipping toward each other in a scrunch of his forehead. He pointed to the guest chair. "Plop a squat."

Shane sat, placed his elbows on the arms of the chair. He didn't know where to begin, how to formulate a thought.

"The days are flying by, that's for sure," Hop offered. "You getting nervous about graduation?"

"Uh, yes, but." He pulled in a lungful of air. "I wanted to run something by you."

"Sure, kid. What's on your mind?"

"Kit."

Hop shoved his glasses up on his head, leaned back

in his chair, and folded his arms across his barrel chest. He blew out a low whistle. "Oh boy, Irish, you're treading in dangerous territory."

He nodded. "I, uh, don't know what to do, Hop. We, Kit and I, we, uh, have been getting close."

"How's that lady over in Paris feeling about that?"

"Dana's in Italy, and we broke up."

"Because of Kit?"

"No. We just realized we weren't meant for each other, I guess. But I'm not going to lie, Hop. I've been developing feelings for Kit since I met her. She's, well, you know, she's a great girl."

"She's been through some rough stuff, son."

"I know."

Hop jabbed his thumb at his chest. "You hurt her, and friend of your father's or not, you'll have to answer to me. You understand?"

Shane nodded.

For a long moment, Hop studied him. "You care about her."

"I do."

A crooked smile slanted Hop's mouth. "She's a piece of work. Ornery when she's upset, snippy when you try to help her." He shook his head. "Stubborn as a mule. But, man, she's got a heart of gold, that girl. She's a keeper. Like I said from day one."

"I'm just not sure how she feels, Hop, or what this is between us. I just don't want to mess it up."

Hop nodded. "Then I think you and that girl need to have a conversation."

Shane smiled at his father's best friend, the one man who knew him longer than anyone. "I wouldn't know what to say."

"Say what's in here." The old man pointed to the center of his chest. "That's the best you can do."

"You're right."

"I'm always right."

Chapter Twenty-Two

That night when Shane pulled his truck into the driveway, Kit's heart did a little dance. He came in through the door with a bouquet of yellow tulips and a bag from the grocery store in his arms. Her heart swelled.

All day her mind had played ping-pong with how things would go from here. Was it a mistake? Was it a beginning for them? She still didn't know, but just seeing his smile and the flowers sent warmth flooding through her. Maybe this could be the start of something good, wonderful even. Maybe.

"For you."

She accepted the tulips and thanked him. "What's in the bag?"

"I thought I'd make you dinner."

"I thought you said you don't cook."

His mouth slanted. "Does English-muffin pizza count?"

She laughed. "I like English-muffin pizza. So yes."

"Great." He put the bag on the counter. "And look." He withdrew a bottle of white zinfandel.

"Wow." She picked up the bottle and examined the label. She knew this brand. It was one she didn't buy for herself because there was a two in front of its price. "Thank you, Fireman."

He sauntered to her and stood so close she could

smell his earthiness. "I thought about you all day."

"Same here."

"You're not regretting anything?"

She shrugged one shoulder. "Honestly, I go back and forth with wondering if we're jumping the gun on things."

"Is that how it feels in here?" He touched a finger to her chest where her heartbeat quickened.

"Not at the moment." Her mouth curved into a smile.

"Okay, let's go with that." He turned back to the bag on the counter and unloaded his purchases, a package of English muffins, a jar of pizza sauce, some shredded mozzarella. "Now let the maestro perform his masterpiece."

"I'll make us a salad." She went to the fridge and pulled open the crisper drawer. "Just so you know, I recorded a movie that was on the thriller channel."

He stopped what he was doing. "What movie?"

"The original *Invasion of the Body Snatchers*."

"The 1956 one?" He sounded like it was Christmas morning.

She nodded. "With Kevin McCarthy."

"Oh, baby," he whooped. "To what do I owe this special specialness?"

For being you. She didn't say it; the words were almost too scary to even think them. But what she did say was "To thank you for coming with me tomorrow."

"Ah," he said. "The bridal shower. What's a Jack and Jill shower again?"

"It's where bridezilla and Brian are showered with gifts together."

"Didn't these parties used to be for women only?"

"Yup."

"I mean, what's a guy care about slow cookers or mixing bowls?"

"Apparently, Brian does."

He shook his head. "So we have to sit around while they open up all that kind of stuff."

"We do."

"You might owe me more than a vintage monster movie there, lady."

A crooked smile claimed her mouth. "I can put croutons on the salad. Does that count?"

His mouth twisted sideways, but his eyes danced. "That's a start."

"Open the wine, Fireman."

Her landline rang, and she peered at the display. "It's Hop." She connected the call. "Hi."

"I need your help."

Hop was never the one to ask for help other than needing a button sewed back on his uniform or to borrow and eventually take ownership of her wine opener. And his voice sounded urgent. A squeezing sensation filled her chest.

"What is it, Hop?"

"You have to come over here and see this. I'm in trouble."

"Be right there."

She hung up and turned to Shane. "Come on. Something's up with Hop."

They hurried out of the house, the screen door slapping loudly behind them. They trotted over to Hop's house, and after a quick rap of her knuckles on the door, they went right in.

"Hop?" She and Shane charged down the hallway

to the kitchen. He wasn't there. "Hop?"

"Out here."

His voice came from outside the sliders that led to his deck, and she'd been wrong when she thought he sounded distressed. He sounded aggravated, which was much more like the old guy. The clench in her chest eased.

Hop sat on the deck's built-in bench, a beer in his hand and a cardboard box at his feet. He was talking to the box. "Don't look at me like that." He shook his head. "You can give me that face all day, and I won't care." He swigged his beer. "*Capish?*"

"Um." She and Shane exchanged a look. This was either comical, or Hop had lost his marbles. "Whatcha doing?"

He pointed the neck of his bottle to the box.

"What's in it?"

"Trouble with a capital *T*."

She and Shane closed the gap between them and peered into the box. A gray kitten with one white tip on the end of its tail looked up at them with milky dark eyes. It emitted a pathetic mew.

A squeal shot from her mouth, and she fell to her knees. "Hello, little guy. How cute are you?"

She reached a hand into the box and petted the fluffy creature. She raised her gaze to meet Hop's. "You call this an *emergency?*"

"I never said *emergency*. I said *trouble*."

Shane crouched next to her and peered at the kitten. "Where'd he come from, Hop?"

"He was crying out on the deck. I didn't know what was making the racket when I first heard it. I gave it some water, but I think it might be sick or something.

It hasn't tried to get out of the box or anything. Maybe he's rabid. What the hell do I know from cats?" He called on a trio of saints—Jesus, Mary, and Joseph—and downed the rest of his beer.

Shane reached in and scooped up the little kitten into his hands. It mewed at him as he cradled the small body against him. He turned it over to reveal a white underside.

"Careful, Irish. He could be sick." Hop called on the trio again, punctuating it with "I need this like I need a hole in my head."

Kit shook her head. "Hop, it's just a little kitten. We can bring it to the animal shelter."

"Then what? If he's sick, they'll put him down. If he's not sick, they'll hope someone comes along to adopt it. And if not, it's curtains for him." He blew out a breath. "How am I supposed to do that to the poor pathetic-looking thing?"

She eyed the kitten in Shane's hold. His big hand was gentle as it ran back and forth over the small body. Her heart melted.

"Helloooooo."

Kit stiffened at the sound of her mother's voice coming from the front of the house. What was Mom doing here?

"Oh God, now what?" Hop stood.

She and Shane exchanged a look. "She must have gone to our place and then figured we were here." She went through inside the house and hurried to the front door. God, she hoped her mother didn't walk through her cottage when she was next door. One look at the loft and she'd figure it out that she and Shane were sleeping apart, that he was just a roommate, not the love of her life, as Mom thought. *Shit, shit, shit.*

Mom stood at Hop's door. She must have been to the hair salon today. Her hair was a different shade. Suddenly her mother was a redhead.

Kit opened the door. "Hi, Mom. You, uh, you changed your hair."

Mom reached up and gave the spiky ends of her hair a quick flip. "You like?"

"Yes, wow, you look…"

"Snazzy?"

Kit laughed. She could conjure no adjective to describe her mother's new do and was glad to be off the hook. "Yes, indeed, Mom. You look snazzy."

"Kicky."

"That, too."

"What are you doing here with that awful man?"

Mom and Hop didn't much get along. She didn't appreciate his gruffness, her refinement lost on the salty old guy. Nothing she said ever impressed good old Hop, and that just irked her like a toothache.

"We're out on his deck. He found a kitten."

"Hunh." Mom stepped into the entryway.

She needed to stall her mother so she and Shane could stage the house to appear as though they were truly a couple. There was only one way to get her mother to stay behind with Hop while they did the switcheroo, and that was to call on Mom's ever-ready need to rescue.

"Mom." The joy of knowing swirled in Kit's chest. "Can you help? Hop's frantic, and Shane and I don't know what to do with a kitten. And it might be sick."

If Mom carried a cape in her designer handbag, now was one of those moments when she'd don it. Her mouth opened, and her eyes widened. She charged past Kit, calling out to her as she went down the hall. "Let me see this poor thing. For God's sake, it's just a baby. And that oaf better not be manhandling it."

When she and Mom went out onto the deck, Shane still held the animal.

"Hello, Shane." Mom cast a disdainful glance at Hop. "Hello."

"Hey, you're a redhead."

Mom lifted her chin to him.

"I like it." Hop came up to her and peered close, as if he were trying to figure out a Picasso painting. "Kind of like Woody Woodpecker."

Her mother's mouth dropped open.

Kit's insides knotted. The last thing she needed was for her mother to stomp away. She gave Hop a subtle pinch on the arm. He mouthed an *ow*.

He cleared his throat. "But red's my favorite color, so I approve."

"As if I care that you do or do not approve." Mom turned her attention to the kitten in Shane's arms. "Let me take a look at this poor baby."

"Careful, Red, it could be rabid," Hop warned. "If you get rabies, we might have to shoot you."

She flashed Hop a narrowed gaze, then turned back to lift the kitten into her arms. She cooed to it, as Kit knew she would.

Kit reached for Shane's hand and gave it a heavy squeeze. She cleared her throat. "Mom, Shane and I need to go check on, um, dinner. We were in the middle of getting things started when Hop called for us to come over."

"What about this little guy? We can't just leave

him, and I'm certainly not staying here without you." She eyed Hop with disdain to which he shrugged, *suit yourself* plastered on his kisser.

"Want a beer?"

Mom clucked her tongue. "I don't drink beer." Her tone was acid, as if Hop had offered her a glass of drain cleaner.

Mom, can you just lose the crown for once, please?

"Mom, we'll be back in a few minutes. Stay put."

"Ten minutes, then I come looking for you."

She pushed Shane toward the door before he could ask any questions. When they were down the hallway, a hot whisper came from her lips. "Quick. We've got to work fast."

Chapter Twenty-Three

Shane and Kit darted up the stairs to the loft and hurriedly worked together to gather his things.

Shane balled up his furry Mets bed throw. "We can shove this in the closet."

"No." Kit put a hand to the furry ball. "Let's put this thing on my bed. For effect."

Shane laughed. "We're getting good at this."

"That's not really a compliment, is it?"

"Desperate measures."

In no time the room had been stripped, as if he'd never been there. Her mind reeled. Everything about this felt lousy now. She was getting good at deception, and she hated herself for it. But there was no undoing it now.

"I'll get the stuff from my bathroom and bring it downstairs."

"Okay." She headed toward the stairs. "Put some of your toiletries on the counter down there, too."

Back in the kitchen she opened the package of English muffins. Shane came up beside her. "I told my mother we were in the middle of preparing dinner. Can you get the cookie sheet out from the drawer under the stove?"

They worked in silence, partners in crime that they were. Shane found a vase in the cabinet under her sink, put the tulips into it, and placed the arrangement on the kitchen table. She was dizzy with the swirling of truth and lies. Right now she didn't know what to think or feel, what to believe. She ladled a dollop of the jarred tomato sauce onto each open English muffin and sprinkled shredded cheese on top.

"You know it's been a lot longer than ten minutes." Shane leaned against the counter.

Kit checked her fitness tracker. A half hour had gone by.

"Wow. I can't believe Mom's still over there. I hope she and Hop haven't killed each other."

He laughed. "Yeah, they seem to be oil and water. How come?"

She looked out the window to see if her mom's car was still in the driveway, which is was. "Still over there. As I'm sure you've picked up on, my mother is kind of hoity-toity, God love her. You'd think she was born and raised on a satin pillow. Her father's family was upper crust, but she and my dad were basically your average middle-of-the-road couple. My dad was an insurance salesman who did house painting on the side for extra money. My mom worked part-time in my school library. But she's always been fastidious, well spoken, well read, and painfully opinionated. But don't get me wrong. She's a good soul."

"I can see that, too. She is very protective of you. I know that much." An easy smile claimed his mouth, which looked good enough to kiss.

"Yeah, she's over the top with that, too. But when she first met Hop, he wasn't her type of human. You know Hop. He pulls no punches, he thinks his jokes are funny, and he can get under your skin if you let him."

"Heart of gold, though."

"Yes sir. And that could be the one thing he and my mother have in common, not that it matters. But maybe we should go over there and see what the holdup is."

She covered the doctored English muffins with foil. Shane put the cheese and leftover sauce in the fridge. The house phone rang. Mom.

"Uh-oh." Kit picked up the receiver. "How's it going over there, Mom?"

"We're not there. That's why I'm calling."

She looked out the window again. Mom's car was there. "Where are you?"

"I'm with Hop. We're taking Smokey to a friend of his who's a vet. The kind man offered to take a look at the baby at his house."

Smokey? She named the kitten?

"Will you please drive slower," Mom said to her escort. "You drive like a maniac."

Kit heard Hop's voice in the background. "Oh, I do not."

"I'm bouncing all over the seat, and Smokey's sliding around in the box, you old fool."

"That's the way it is in a truck. But I guess you wouldn't know. Good news is you bounce pretty damn good."

"Of all the nerve."

"Mom? I didn't even hear Hop's truck leave. When did you go?"

"Just now. His truck was in the street for some nonsensical reason."

"Because I blew the leaves off the driveway, if you don't mind."

"Anyway, Kit darling, I'll stop by your house to fill

you in when we get back. I just wanted you to know not to wait for me for dinner. I don't know how long we'll be. We need to have this baby checked out tonight."

"And you're calling him *Smokey*?"

"Well, of course. Hop's a fireman."

In the background Hop laughed. "Where there's smoke, there's fire, Red."

And she wasn't hearing things. She recognized the sound. Her mother was giggling.

When the call ended, she turned to Shane. "Okay, where's the wine?"

Chapter Twenty-Four

The English-muffin pizzas were surprisingly good.

"The extent of my meal-prep ability, I'm afraid. Unless you count heating up leftover takeout." Shane's eyes danced as he looked at her from across the kitchen table.

God, he was appealing. She glanced up at the clock on the wall. It was after nine. How long did it take for a vet to give a kitten a look-see? Mom had said she would stop in when she got back, and until she'd come and seen the pretend coupledom of their living arrangements, Shane's ugly, garish blue Mets throw was staying on her bed. He'd said earlier he was planning to make it an early night, having an early morning meeting at the firehouse tomorrow. She looked at him again. Where was this cute-as-hell fireman going to lay his head tonight?

He cleaned up the paper plates and napkins and put the cookie sheet in the sink. He peered out the window before he turned to face her. "You think they killed each other by now?"

A smile claimed her mouth. Her mother detested— that was her word—Hop, but somehow the old guy had managed to get her mother to giggle. It made no sense. Then again, what did she know about sense?

They tried getting into their movie, the one they had been excited about. But Kit's mind wouldn't stop reeling. Playing this game to fool her family weighed on her tonight like a new and ugly version of an invasion of body snatchers.

By ten o'clock Mom's car was still in the driveway and Hop's truck was not back. Next to her on the couch, Shane yawned.

"You better go to bed." The word *bed* tasted foreign in her mouth. It had been one thing to indulge in lovemaking in the heat of the moment. It was entirely another to lie in bed with a man under the blankets, all cozy. Somehow that felt more intimate.

"It's your call, Kit. If you want me to doze on the sofa, just say the word. When and if your mom stops by, I'll sneak down to your room."

She shook her head. "Not taking a chance at this stage of the game."

****

A little while later Kit lay under the covers with the fireman just inches from her. He smelled like soap, clean. She stared at the ceiling and listened to her foolish heart thudding in her chest. She could hear his even breathing. If she moved her hand just a couple of inches, she could feel his skin.

His words came softly in the darkness. "Kit, I wanted you to know that even though this is the craziest thing I've ever done—" He paused to swallow. "—if I had the chance to do it again, I would. Meeting you has changed everything."

She rolled toward him. "I know I've thanked you for getting involved in this sham, but really, you have been such a good sport."

He turned on his side to face her. His eyes appeared black with the lack of light to illuminate the green of his irises. His hand came up and touched the side of her face.

She wanted to say so many things to him in this moment yet didn't dare. Her heart was rattled, and her mind was pudding. If she learned anything since the debacle of last Christmas Eve, it was to open her eyes. And right now the darkness in this room kept her from seeing anything.

Her doorbell sounded, making her jerk. She sat up. She and Shane paused for a beat and held a look. Then she went to answer the door. Shane followed.

Bright-eyed and smiling, Mom glided in through the door. "Did I wake you two?"

"Um, no, we had just gone to, you know, bed." She swallowed. "How did you make out at the vet? You were gone a long time."

Mom uttered a soft laugh. "The vet was very nice, and he said that although Smokey's a little skinny, he's in tip-top shape. He estimates the kitten is about six or seven weeks old."

"Good news, then," Shane said. "He's a lucky little guy that you and Hop rescued him, huh?"

"Oh." Mom clapped her hands. "Then we went to Walmart and got him everything he needs. A crate, a bed, a litter box, a pooper-scooper, food, and treats, of course."

"So Hop's keeping him?"

Her mother's eyes were a little googly. "That old coot wouldn't let Smokey go to the pound for all the money in China."

"Well, that's nice, Mom. I'm glad you went with him. Maybe you've got a new perspective on Hop, huh?"

"Don't go crazy, Kitrina. He's still an oaf." Mom kissed her on the cheek. "Go back to bed, kids. I'll see you both tomorrow at the shower." That last statement was in singsong.

"Mom, did you get a chance to eat anything for dinner?"

"Oh yes. Hop bought me a hotdog at the snack bar in Walmart. Surprisingly tasty." She turned on her heel and left.

"Could they be finding a friendship?" Shane scratched his head.

"I'd settle for a tolerance."

They held a long gaze. There was no reason now to sleep in the same bed, and they both knew it.

"So I guess we'll just call it a night." The words were meant to come out casual, but she heard the lament in her own tone.

"Guess so."

"I'll get your throw."

"I'll come with you."

"Okay."

Together they walked down the hallway to her bedroom. When their gazes locked, the message in her smoky eyes was clear. He and that fuzzy blue Mets throw wouldn't make it back up to the loft.

Chapter Twenty-Five

The parking lot of the Admiral Hotel downtown was packed, and Shane circled the aisles looking for a space to park his truck. Kit was quiet in the seat beside him, balancing a wrapped gift box on her lap. Although he hadn't actually seen what was inside, she had told him it contained a place setting of the bride and groom's dinnerware of choice. He'd offered to go in on the cost of the gift, but she wasn't having it. Oddly, the dismissal caught him off guard. He kept forgetting that their solid-twosome status was a made-up story for Kit's family. It reminded him what they shared was new, precarious, and maybe even nothing more than a suspended moment in time. What did he know?

He found an empty spot in the back of the parking lot and turned his steering wheel to maneuver into the tight space. Putting the lever in park, he slid his gaze over to Kit. She bit down on her perfect lip. Her fingers, the nail polish a shade of lavender, drummed on the top of the gift she held in her lap.

"Ready?"

Kit blew out a long breath. "As I'll ever be."

He reached over and stilled her hand. "We've got this, Kit. Piece of cake, right?"

She lifted her gaze to meet his. Her eyes shone with trepidation. Was that look all about the shower awaiting them, or was it something else, too? Was he the only one wondering what this was between them? Was she hoping, as he was, they had begun something with lasting possibilities, or was she admonishing herself for what had transpired?

He carried the box up the steps of the hotel and found the room location on the bulletin board set up in the lobby.

Their shoes clicked on the tile floor as they walked to the Acorn Lounge where double doors were open and tables upon tables were occupied with attendees. At the front of the room sat the bride and groom at a little table for two befitting a king and queen of the prom. *Oh brother.*

Kit's mother spied them first. "Over here, kids." She waved and pointed to two chairs next to hers that were tilted forward, claimed. "I saved you seats. Shane, put that gift over there." She motioned toward a mountain, a serious heap of wrapped boxes.

He whistled under his breath. How long would it take to go through all that loot?

Kit introduced him to people at the table, and he managed to participate in polite chitchat while the courses of the luncheon were being served in sequence. Between the salad and the entrée, he leaned over to Kit and whispered in her ear. She smelled of that citrusy perfume she used, and he breathed her in.

"How are you doing? Okay?"

She smiled in response. "You're a trooper, Fireman."

"When do they start opening up that mass of gifts?"

"Any minute now."

He shook his head. "I'm going to grab a beer at the

bar. Can I get you a glass of wine?"

"Just one?"

He laughed and instinctively squeezed her knee under the table. Those spontaneous gestures of intimacy confused him. He tended to forget they really weren't this solid, committed couple all of these people around them thought they were.

"Mrs. Baxter, can I get you something from the bar? A glass of wine, maybe?"

"Oh, that would be lovely, Shane." She flashed an approving look to her daughter. "Such manners."

He left the table and made his way through the crowd.

****

Kit watched as Shane retreated from the room and felt a tug inside her chest. He was a good guy, and she liked him more than she should. He was just off a relationship, and that was dangerous territory. She would not, could not, go through another disappointment. She reached for her water glass and took a gulp. She'd managed to avoid her dinner roll so far, but at the moment it was calling her from the little plate at her place. Was that a Portuguese roll? Were those pats of butter shaped like butterflies made with herbs? She liked herbs. *Carbs will not fix you.*

Co-Co appeared at their table and slipped an easy hand on the back of Kit's mom's chair. "How are you, ladies?"

They exchanged some small talk that Kit managed to zone out until she heard mention of the wedding dress.

"You should see it, Auntie. Kitty-Cat has outdone herself." A gratuitous grin broke out on her face.

"You're a marvel, cousin."

"Thank you." It was all Kit could think to say. A lump had formed in her throat. It was just a dress, her mind chanted. A flush climbed up her neck and flooded her cheeks. Just an old dress. A garment did not hold sentiment. Hearts did. And her heart belonged to her, and no one was going to take it from her.

"If you'll excuse me." She stood and placed her napkin on her chair. "Need to find the restroom."

Thankfully, the corridor outside the dining room blasted her with cold air-conditioning. She could feel the heat dissipating from her cheeks. In the ladies' room she wet a towel and dabbed it on the back of her neck and on her forehead.

Leaving the room, she headed back toward the dining room and ran smack dab into Brian.

"Hey, you," he greeted. He wore a pale-blue collared shirt with white pindots. She liked the fabric, but it didn't fit him well and made his shoulders look scrawny. He appeared thinner. Had his bride-to-be put him on one of her famous diets? She bet he hadn't eaten his dinner roll.

"Hi."

"You look nice." He cast his eyes down her form, and heat rushed to her face. She looked down at the dress she wore as though she'd forgotten what she had on.

"Thanks." An awkward pause hung between them. She needed to fill the space. "Boy, um, you two have a lot of gifts out there, huh?"

"People are generous, that's for sure."

"Well, then..." She took a small step away, and Brian reached out to touch her arm.

"Hey, Kit, can I talk with you a second?"

Her insides stopped. "About what?"

"This guy you're with. Shane. Look, it's none of my business…"

"You're right. It isn't."

"But." He flashed a smile. He'd had his teeth whitened. They were neon like Co-Co's. "I just hope you're not rushing things. I mean, I feel kind of responsible if this is a rebound kind of thing. I know I brought this up before, but it's been on my mind."

"Brian…"

"I'm sure it's not easy dealing with all this, and I hope you're thinking clearly, that's all. I mean, what do you know about this guy? What's he even know about you, Kit?"

"If you have a question about me, why don't you ask me?"

Kit turned to the voice, knowing it was Shane. He closed the space between them and put an arm around her shoulders.

"Hey." Brian shuffled his feet. "I was just asking Kit if she thinks you two are rushing things, that's all. I just wondered how much you two know about each other."

"Brian, I know more about this lady than you ever did."

Brian's mouth quirked. "I doubt that."

"I do."

"You didn't know about her cat, Blue."

"I know what makes her laugh, what makes her cry. I know what makes her jump for joy. Do you know why she likes the color *teal*? I personally think it's a stupid color—no offense, babe—but it's not green, and it's not blue. It's kind of both. But that's why she likes it. She likes it because it's the result of two things coming together."

"Um…"

"And what's she scared of more than anything?"

Brian looked from Kit to Shane.

"Spiders. She's terrified of spiders. Does she drink coffee or tea? Coffee. She likes it dark and sweet. What's her weakness? Anything with flour in it. Her favorite movie? She's got two—*Gone with the Wind* and *Invasion of the Body Snatchers*. The old one made in 1956. She takes vitamins, the chewable kind because she hates swallowing pills. She wears a size seven shoe, and she hates heels. She's allergic to penicillin. Gives her a rash. She loves guitar and wishes she knew how to play."

"Wow." Brian put his hands up in surrender. "Okay. Point taken."

"Ready, babe?" He tightened his arm around her shoulder.

On the way back to the Acorn Lounge, Kit and Shane did not speak. They didn't need to. He gave her hand a squeeze, and she returned the gesture.

Chapter Twenty-Six

Parts of the event felt like an out-of-body experience, especially watching Brian, the man she had known, the explorer type who had a world map on the wall in his living room with colored pushpins jabbed into all the exotic locations he wanted to see. Where was that guy? Where was the man who wanted to hike mountains and camp on the land? She watched him *oohing* and *ahhing* over serving trays and ice buckets and thought for sure the body snatchers were running rampant in Sycamore River.

Co-Co was in her element today, however. All the attention, all the gifts, all the very air in the room belonged to her. She yelped over bedsheets and matching duvet covers. She pressed bath towels to her face and moaned in delight. "Here, Bri-Bri, feel how soft," she said as she pressed the fern-green terry fabric to his cheek.

Shane leaned in close to Kit's ear with a whisper that tickled her skin. "He's Bri-Bri now?"

She turned to face him.

His eyes danced. "Is it a prerequisite that they all have double names?"

She covered her mouth to suppress the laugh that threatened to escape.

After all the gifts were opened and the cake was cut, she was thankful she and Shane could say their goodbyes and get out of there.

Sitting in the passenger seat of Shane's truck, she turned to him. "Thanks for enduring the shower."

He shook his head. "That was quite an event, huh? They're not going to have to spend a dime on a thing."

"Crazy, right?"

"Did it bother you to see Brian amidst all that hoopla?"

She paused before answering. She kept envisioning the world map on Brian's wall. "Bother? No. Seeing him in that scene seemed so foreign from the guy I knew. It's like he abandoned who he was and what he planned for his future." She tilted her head. "He must love her that much, I guess."

"That doesn't sound like love to me. Not the way I see it, anyway."

She studied him, the memory of Shane coming to her defense when Brian targeted her appearing in her mind. "About what you said to Brian."

He nodded as he kept his eyes on the road ahead of him.

She continued. "How'd you know all those things about me? I mean, I know we crammed with details of ourselves, but we did not cover all that."

"Is that okay?"

She uttered a soft, nervous laugh. "It's just that I didn't realize how transparent I can be."

"You're not transparent, Kit. I just pay attention."

Her heart whirred in her chest. This man who had come out of nowhere, this good sport who had agreed to play along with a ruse to fool her family, was finding his way into her heart, and it scared the hell out of her. She turned to look out the passenger window. The trees and mailboxes whizzed by. They moved so fast it made her dizzy.

****

Back at the house, Kit kicked off her shoes and padded into the kitchen to grab a bottle of water. She went to the sink with her water and sipped as her eyes focused on the group of trees outside and the sight of the river beyond them. It was a dusky hour, and a purplish hue seeped into every cranny of the space in the woods, consuming every inch, all encompassing. The lyrics to a John Denver song wafted through her mind.

Another sip was a relief, the coolness sliding down through her. Still, she and every single cell of her body were acutely aware Shane Dugan was there in the room. All she had to do was turn to him.

The sound of his cell phone jarred her, yet she didn't flinch or turn away from her view of the outside. Not that she was into eavesdropping, but even after he had stepped away, his footfalls sounding on the hardwood as he strode into the living room, she heard his responses to the conversation coming at him from the phone.

"No, that's not how things are. No. Absolutely not. Where's this coming from?" An agonizingly long pause came next, and then he continued. "Okay, you too, Dana. Yes. Of course. Bye."

When the call ended, silence filled the space in the house like the purple presence of nightfall outside. The only sound she heard was the swallow of water traveling down her throat. *Dana.* The call had been from Dana. What had his responses meant? *Absolutely not* what? *Of course* what? Her mind was a zigzag.

Shane's footsteps sounded as he approached, and at last she turned to him.

"Don't ask me how, but Dana has heard that I'm dating."

"What?"

"Yeah, someone from home must have seen you and me, is all I can think of."

"She didn't react well to that?" Kit already surmised the answer to her own question, but she didn't want him to know she'd been not just listening but assessing the words that came out of his mouth in response to Dana.

"No, but it doesn't change anything. She and I are on different wavelengths. There's no debating that."

Suddenly the space between them was too thick, and her lungs suffered for air. "I, uh, was going to head over to Rylee's for a while."

She put the water bottle on the counter and moved to grab her purse.

Shane just stood there with his eyes on her.

She searched the pouch for her key.

"Kit…"

She pulled the key out with a flourish. "I hate these small purses." She slipped her feet back into her shoes. "You can lock up. I'm not sure how long I'll be." She made her way to the door.

"Hey." He came up to her. "You okay?"

She laughed a tone that sounded foreign. "Sure. I just wanted to touch base with Rylee about this woman she's meeting with that has a business deal to talk with her about. Rylee originally asked me to join them, but I told her we had the shower. Since we're back early enough, I thought I'd pop by."

"Okay."
They held a long gaze. "Night."
And she was gone.

Chapter Twenty-Seven

Shane left the light on in the kitchen and climbed the stairs up to the loft, his feet heavy. His conversation with Dana swirled around in his head, mingling with the memory of Kit's eyes when she looked at him as she left to see her friend.

He still didn't understand what Dana's call was about. She was angry and wouldn't elaborate on how she'd learned he was seeing someone. She'd accused him of two-timing her all along, and that was what hung heavy in him tonight. He was not a cheater, and the moment he'd realized his feelings for Kit, he owned that. Maybe Dana was projecting her own situation onto him. After all, he'd spied the man's watch on Dana's nightstand and the two glasses of water by the bed. And somebody had been behind that door of her bathroom.

He brushed his teeth, washed up with rote moves, his mind too occupied to think straight. Discomfort jabbed at him like a sharp point to his gut. He did not like offending Dana or anyone, even if it was something fabricated in their own head. He wasn't that guy. Raising Nick those years must have cemented a sense of responsibility in his DNA, and maybe that had been the birth of his ingrained need to rescue.

He shut the light in the bathroom and crossed the room to his bed, where he sank onto the mattress. He needed to cool his own jets and ignore the knifepoint poking at him. Dana and her lashing out did not need his rescuing. He did hope, though, he'd quelled her accusation so they could both move on.

He stared at the ceiling, hands tucked behind his head, and waited for the sound of Kit returning home, but sleep won him over first.

Chapter Twenty-Eight

Rylee's appointment with a former Rosie's Bridals' bride, Megan, was already underway when Kit arrived at the apartment. Rylee's fiancé was there as well.

Darius and Rylee had an obvious ease about them. Their love for each other all but telegraphed itself to everyone in their company, a touch to a shoulder, a smile from across the room. Kit saw all of it as if her radar had been awakened, her nerve endings like transmitters of matters of the heart.

But tonight whenever Shane came to mind, she was reminded of his phone call from Dana. She couldn't wait to get her best friend's take on it, but it would be a while before this meeting was over and she could get Rylee alone.

Megan had lost her husband two years before and had been one of the former brides who participated in the fashion show last year. She was a beautiful woman with a sadness in her blue eyes so apparent it could stop someone dead. But her smile was a brave one, an infectious one, and Kit found herself smiling back.

"Megan, you look wonderful."

"You're all too kind. Thank you."

"So, Rylee, catch me up." Kit took a seat on the sofa beside Megan. Rylee and Darius sat in chairs that faced the couch. There were teacups on the table and a pot of tea.

"Help yourself to some tea, Kit." Rylee handed her an empty cup.

She waved her off. She was too jumpy for tea.

Rylee pointed to a bundle of plastic-covered garments bent over the dining table across the room. "Darius helped Megan bring the dresses over."

"There are twenty," Megan said. "And each one is prettier than the next. Granted, they need some TLC."

"That's where the genius of Kit Baxter comes in." Darius flashed a smile.

The dresses were vintage wedding gowns Megan was giving to Rosie's Bridals. She was taking over a space downtown where a second-hand shop had been housed. The store went out of business, and she was about to embark on reopening, concentrating on furniture and estate jewelry, not clothing.

"You must be so excited, Megan," Kit offered.

"I'm thinking it's more like hysteria, but yeah, it's got me jazzed."

"When do you anticipate opening your shop?"

"There's a lot of work yet to do."

"If there's anything we can do to help you, give a holler." Darius was a good resource, and Kit was glad he made the offer. Megan just made you want to root for her.

Kit got up from the sofa and went to the dresses, and Rylee joined her. They flipped the dry-cleaner bags up to hug the neck of the hanger as they inspected each dress. Some were in better shape than others, but all twenty vintage wedding gowns were salvageable.

"Megan, these are wonderful." Rylee's eyes misted, and in turn Kit's did as well.

Rosie's Bridals belonged to her friend, but Kit was as invested in it and in Rylee as she could be. "Are you sure we can't pay you for them?"

"All I hope is that they wind up in the hands of happy brides."

"This is going to really give Rosie's a new burst of life, Megan." Rylee put a hand to her chest.

"And we're going to advertise the hell out of our new division." Darius put a hand out and slid it across an imaginary banner. "Rosie's Vintage Couture."

Megan clasped her hands. "How wonderful."

"And you can count on us to help you get your shop launched." He lifted his water bottle. "To our contribution to keeping Sycamore River's downtown the quaint village it's always been."

****

After Megan left and Darius went into another room to get some work done, Kit seized the opportunity to get Rylee's opinion about Shane's phone call from Dana.

Rylee tilted her head in contemplation. "Did you ask him about it?"

"No. I figured if there was something he wanted me to know, he'd have said." Kit leaned her head back against the sofa cushion and spoke to the ceiling. "What am I doing, Ry?"

"You're feeling it out, friend."

She rolled her head to meet Rylee's gaze. "We must not forget that I'm an idiot."

"We're talking about Mr. Maybe, I presume."

"This pretend boyfriend story is backfiring on me. It's like I made up a nice little world and then moved right in. That's how it feels tonight anyway."

"That phone call probably meant nothing. Don't project what Brian did onto this guy."

"I know. Shane couldn't be more different from Brian. That much I do know. The rest?" She shrugged. "The wedding is soon. After that who knows what will happen?"

****

The house was dark when she returned home. She was disappointed. Somehow she just wished she'd had a chance to talk with Shane, see his face. She was falling for him. Her heart was still tender, and each pang felt like a jackhammer, but still she could not deny Shane had given her the hope she had sworn not to feel. Was it just weeks ago he sat at Hop's kitchen table for the first time? Had she known then how she'd feel now, would she have agreed to this arrangement? The answer was yes. At least she could admit the truth.

After putting on her pajamas, she went into the kitchen for a drink of water. She stood at her favorite spot and looked out the glass pane into the night. The lights were on in Hop's house. She wondered how he was doing with Smokey.

She looked at the display on her fitness tracker. It was after midnight. What was he doing up at this hour? Was the kitten okay? Should she call him?

Shoving her feet into a pair of garden clogs and tugging on her college sweatshirt, Kit slipped out the door. She crunched over the gravel toward Hop's stoop and peered into the small window on the door. Hop sat with his back to her at the kitchen table. She swallowed and rapped on the door. Instantly, he turned and saw her.

He lumbered down his hallway and opened the

door. "What are you doing here at this hour?"

"Why are you up at this hour?"

"Do you ever answer a question?"

"Do you?"

"Oh for God's sake, kid, you coming in or what?"

She followed him into his kitchen. An empty glass sat on the table next to a bottle of scotch. A newspaper was splayed on the surface.

"How's the kitten?"

"He's sleeping on my goddamn bed." A rueful smile curved one side of his mouth. "Little fur ball." He studied Kit. "Have a seat. Can I get you anything?"

She unzipped her sweatshirt and sat next to him. "You have chamomile tea?"

He scrunched his face. "Do I look like I'd have tea made out of dead flowers?"

She shook her head. "Never mind." She pointed to the empty glass. "Looks like you've already had a beverage."

"You got a problem with that?"

"What keeps you up tonight, old man?"

He twisted his mouth sideways. "They want me to retire."

"What? Who does?"

"The town. The department. It's past my expiration date, I guess." He laughed, but there was no humor in the sound.

Kit surveyed the newspaper on the table. It was open to the classified section, which in this small town wasn't even a half a column long.

"You looking for a new job, Hop?"

"No. Maybe. There's nothing anyway unless I want to sell solar panels to unsuspecting patsies." He scoffed.

"Or replacement windows. There's nothing for me in here."

"Is there some kind of age limit on being in the fire department?"

"Not to be a volunteer member, but to be a paid officer, yeah, you can't be older than seventy. I'm seventy-two."

"Oh."

"Don't get old, kid."

Her heart lurched for this man who had grown to mean so much to her. "You know, Hop, maybe it wouldn't be so bad. You could do all the things you like. Kayaking on the river, tinkering on things around here, and didn't you say you've always wanted to buy a trailer and take it cross-country? Maybe now's the time."

A wry smile claimed his mouth. "That's what Ellie and I wanted to do. It was our dream."

She didn't know what to say to that. What did one do when they had a dream that included someone else who was no longer here?

"Every single minute I'd be wishing Ellie was there with me." He turned to her with shiny eyes. "I still miss her."

"I know."

"Ellie and me, we were happy. Don't get me wrong, kid. We fought like hell sometimes." He grinned. "She always won, but that's beside the point." He poured a scant amount of the brown liquid into his glass and chugged it. "We had everything. Look around you. See this little place with the cracks in the ceiling and the damn moody plumbing? We were as happy as if this was a palace."

"Sounds—" Kit swallowed the lump that had formed in her throat. "—sounds lovely."

"Kid, if you ever listen to anything I say, listen now. The right partner means everything. All the other stuff, the bills, the worries, the ups and downs, they mean zilch when you've got the right person at your side. The problem, though, is if they leave you." He shook his head. "That damn cancer beat us both up, I'll tell you."

She pushed up from the chair and went to the cabinet where Hop kept his drinking glasses. She withdrew a glass that matched his, came back to the table, and poured herself a little of the scotch. She hated scotch, but right now it was all she could think to do. She swigged, then grimaced and coughed. She slammed her glass down. "Bleh."

Hop chuckled. "Lightweight."

"I drink pink wine, Hop, not this battery acid."

"Yeah, and tea made out of weeds." He shook his head. "You're a piece of work."

"Hop, I think the right next chapter will come to you. Give yourself a little time to let the dust settle, and it'll hit you. You'll see."

"You think so?"

"I do."

"Here's the thing, I guess. When a new chapter starts, you have to go for it. Believe it's going to be a good one. If you don't believe, you'll never achieve. I didn't make that up. It's on a poster at the firehouse."

All she could do was nod.

"How are you doing, kid?"

"You were right. I am a piece of work."

"You feeling like him over there?" He motioned

his head in the direction of her house. "You starting to like the guy?"

"What do you mean, *feeling like him*?" Her heart whirred in her chest.

"He came to talk to me, but you didn't hear this from me, you understand?"

"He went to see you? About me?"

"He's sweet on you." A teasing light came into his dark eyes. "No accounting for taste."

She punched her fist into his thick shoulder. "What did he say exactly?"

"My lips are sealed."

"Since when?"

"Come on, Kit. I said too much already. Let's just say the guy's thinking about what's going to happen once this wedding happens."

"That makes two of us."

"I still can't believe you roped that poor guy into a charade." Hop folded up the newspaper. "Now I know where you get it from. That mother of yours roping me into this nonsense with a little cat. Don't get me started."

"Careful, Hop. Before you know it, you and Mom are going to be buddies."

He slapped the newspaper. "Okay, you. Time to call it a night. Past my bedtime. I'm as old as dirt, apparently."

He pushed up from the chair and carried his glass to the sink. She followed and placed her glass beside his. Standing there at his sink, she put her head on Hop's shoulder, an impulse that surprised her. "You're not past your expiration date, Hop. Not to me."

"Thanks, kid." He placed an arm around her

shoulders and briefly tucked her close. "Starting over stinks."

She nodded. "Like garbage."

Chapter Twenty-Nine

Kit woke the next morning with a vivid memory of last night's dream. She was on the river in a yellow kayak, paddling with gusto, her arms aching with the effort. She was chasing something, or something was chasing her. She woke panting.

Since it was only five in the morning, too early to get ready for work, she got up, shrugged into her flannel robe, and strode into the kitchen to make a cup of coffee. She cast a glance to the loft and guessed Shane was gone already. She looked out the window to the driveway. His missing truck confirmed her suspicion.

She toasted herself a bagel. While she waited for it to be browned just right, she had a good rebellious feeling watching the heat bars toast the carbohydrates that would soon be her breakfast. The wedding date was creeping up on her, and she hadn't lost all the eight pounds she'd put on since Christmas. On a good day the wretched bathroom scale said she was down half of them. Most days, three. Today "so what" sat on her lips, and it tasted sweet. She was done trying to fit herself into someone else's mold or someone else's cocktail dress.

She spread a light coating of cream cheese on the too-hot bagel and took a bite of the edge so as not to burn the roof of her mouth. She ate half and tossed the rest in the trash. Her mind was on Shane. She wished he were home so she could tell him about her visit with Hop and his having to suddenly come up with a new path for himself.

The conversation would wait until later. Shane had said he was coming home right after work to study for the upcoming test. Maybe she'd make dinner for the two of them. Something celebratory. She'd even stop off at Danziger's Bakery after work and get a fudge brownie for them to share. To hell with the phone call from Dana that had had her worried. She was sick to the point of nausea of overthinking everything. For once she was just going to go with her feelings, ride them out, as if she were in Hop's yellow kayak.

She knew it now—she hadn't been running from anything in her dream. She'd been rushing toward Shane. And tonight, God help her and her urge to fish out the other half of that bagel from the trash can, she was going to tell it all to the fireman.

Chapter Thirty

That night Kit got home later than she'd wanted. The grocery store had been a mob scene, and traffic through town did not cooperate after her pit stop at the bakery. When she pulled into the driveway, Shane's truck wasn't there, and she was glad for the chance to get dinner started. She hoped she could pull off the meal since she'd never made the recipe before.

He'd told her that one of the guys at the firehouse made pasta carbonara, and she'd found a doable recipe on the internet. Apparently, it was all in the technique.

She unloaded her wares and took out her deep-frying pan. She stuck the six-pack of beer on the fridge shelf, chilled the wine she bought, and set the table.

The impulse buy of a bunch of daffodils made her happy. She arranged them in a vase and put them on the table.

She went into her room and changed into jeans and a blue button-down shirt. She rolled the cuffs up to her elbow as she stepped into the bathroom. She fussed with her hair, spritzed some fragrance at her neck, and applied lip gloss. Before she doused the bathroom light, she heard Shane's truck, the tires crunching on the gravel the telltale sign. Her heart giddyupped in her chest. Boldness felt good yet scary. She pulled in a deep breath. She remembered her dream of the kayak. *If you don't work the oars, you'll be at the mercy of the river.*

She would no longer let an outside force be her guide.

She walked down the hallway and found Shane in the kitchen. The look on his face was not what she'd expected. In her mind's eye she'd seen his broad smile and his bright eyes. She even imagined him pulling her into his arms and twirling her around with ease, as though she were as weightless as a feather.

The Shane standing in front of her was not that guy. His mouth was pressed into a seam, and his eyes glinted with a kind of confusion. Suddenly she felt silly. She wished she'd skipped the daffodils. They sat on the table with their heads bowed as though even they felt embarrassed.

"What's, uh, what's all this?" Shane put his messenger bag on the floor and took a step closer. "Are you expecting company?"

"Um..."

"It's okay if you are, because, um, I have to go out anyway."

"Oh."

"Kit, there's something I have to tell you."

"Okay." Her heart stammered in her chest.

"Dana's here."

"Here?" She swallowed hard despite her parched throat. "What do you mean here?"

"She flew in on a red-eye last night. She's at her apartment in Mountain Lakes."

"Did you know she was coming?"

"No clue."

"Is she, um, home for good?"

"I don't even know. I guess I'll find out, though. She wants to see me. Tonight."

Right now she wished she were in that kayak so

she could flip it over and drown her stupid self.

He closed the distance between them. "Kit, I had no idea she was coming. But it doesn't change anything for me anyway. I just want you to know that."

She nodded, too afraid to open her mouth for fear of what she might say.

"You believe me?"

Suddenly all she could see was that mistletoe hanging from a thumbtack on the molding above Aunt Dee Dee's dining room doorway. The snapshot of Brian holding Co-Co in his arms hung in her head like in a frame. There was no way she'd let herself go through anything like that again. Ever.

Her gaze slid to Shane's. Worry shone moist in his eyes. Shane was not Brian. She had long established that. Did she believe him? What was it Hop had said about taking a chance and believing? *If you don't believe, you'll never achieve.*

"Yes." She forced a smile she didn't feel. "I believe you."

"Good." His beautiful mouth curved into a smile.

"What time are you meeting her?"

He checked his watch. "Whoa, I better get ready."

He hurried through the rooms to the loft, leaving her alone with the sound of his quick footfalls on the steps.

****

Shane had no idea what to expect. He stepped into the dark interior of Jabberwocky's and scanned the room. Dana wasn't here yet. His friend Larry from the academy was at the bar drinking a beer.

"Hey, Larry."

Larry swiveled a quarter turn on his stool and

extended his hand. "Irish." He motioned toward the empty stool next to him. "We've got to stop meeting like this. Let me buy you a beer."

"Thanks anyway. I'm meeting someone."

"One of your lady friends?"

He blew out a lungful of air. He didn't like the implication that he had a couple of women on a string. But he wasn't going to make an issue out of it.

Larry chuckled. "Don't ever play poker, buddy. Not with that face."

Dana walked in through the revolving door. She was dolled up in a clingy raspberry-colored dress, a long multicolored scarf trailing down the front of her. Her long brown hair was windblown and cascaded around her shoulders. She was a looker, that was for sure.

"That one of them?"

"Her name's Dana." He waved a hand. "Dana, over here."

Larry tucked his head and spoke low. "Which one is this one? The original or the new one?"

"Original."

"Damn."

Dana came up to him and threw her arms around him. She squeezed close. Her perfume smelled heavy, as if she'd drenched herself in a bucket of flowers. He was reminded of the yellow flowers sitting in the glass jar on Kit's table. She'd never said who was coming over for dinner.

Dana pulled away and held him at arm's length. "Look at you." Her gaze traveled down his body in a slow, deliberate scan.

Larry poked his head in between them. "I'm Larry,

one of this guy's friends at the academy. Just so you know, I've taught him everything he knows."

"Have you?" She proffered a coy smile, and Shane recognized the playful lilt in her voice. "I'm Dana."

"A pleasure to meet you, Dana." Larry's voice was syrupy sweet.

"We're going to get a table, Larry. I'll see you tomorrow."

"Enjoy, kids."

He followed Dana to the hostess stand, and they were seated at a table and given menus. They ordered drinks, a beer for him and a glass of red wine for her.

"Shane, it's so good to see you," she said when the waitress walked away. "Really good."

"You're looking well."

"I'm looking well? Don't you mean hot?" She tilted her head provocatively. "Tell me I'm hot."

A flush of heat climbed up his face. He was confused. What was this about? He took a sip of his beer. "Dana…"

She leaned in close. "I came all this way to see you. At least tell me you're glad I came. Are you happy to see me?"

"I'm, um, confused actually, Dana. Why are you here?"

"Don't you know?"

He shook his head.

"You, Shane. I'm here for you."

Chapter Thirty-One

Jabberwocky's was crowded, but it always was at this hour. Kit made her way through the throng toward the bar. Every seat was taken. She hovered close, hoping she'd get lucky and a couple of seats would become available before Rylee got there.

A man at the corner was paying his tab, and she inched closer to him. She could see others eyeing the coveted stools around the bar. He threw a couple of bills onto the wooden surface, pushed the stool back, and stood. When he turned around, she recognized him from when she'd gone to the firehouse to see Hop.

"It's all yours." He motioned a hand to the seat.

"Thank you."

"Hey, aren't you the friend of Hop's?"

"I am. Larry, right?"

Suddenly his face fell. "You're the one that, uh, Shane Dugan's renting a room from."

"I am."

She wondered why he looked like that.

"Then you must be the pretend one, right? Man, that guy's one lucky son of a bitch, I'll tell you that."

"Excuse me? *The pretend* what?"

He wiped the smile from his face. "I'm sorry. I've had a couple of beers and don't know how to keep my mouth shut sometimes."

Her face flamed. She wished he'd go and prayed

Rylee would walk through the door.

Her insides clenched as she repeated her question. "What did you mean, though? The *pretend* what?"

"Girlfriend. He told me about your arrangement. But don't worry. I can keep a secret even if I've got a big mouth. But, yeah, he's here with the real one. I mean the other one." He pointed to the dining room.

Her heart fell and landed at her feet, like a stone chipped and cracked from its sudden fall. Despite her head chanting for her to get the hell out of the place, she cast her gaze to the dining room, and there they were. Shane had his hand extended across the small square table as he held Dana's hand.

She turned around to find Rylee standing behind her. "Parking around the square's nuts tonight." She studied Kit's face. "Now that I'm here, can you tell me what's going on? Your text concerned me. I mean, aren't you supposed to be making spaghetti carbonara for your fireman?" Rylee sounded confused. "What are we doing at Jabberwocky's?"

She looked into the dining room again. The couple was standing now, and Dana, small and fit, was in Shane's embrace. She craned her neck, lifted her hands up to his cheeks, and pulled his head closer to hers. She planted a kiss, and his hands went to her teeny-tiny waist. Kit's insides turned to cement, and her lungs suffered for air despite her attempts to suck some in.

"Kit."

She'd forgotten for a second that Rylee was even there. All she could do was stare at her friend.

"Sweetie, what's going on?"

"I can't."

"Tell me."

"Not here. Let's go."

"Go? Go where?"

"Anywhere but here."

Chapter Thirty-Two

Shane gently pushed Dana away to disengage the kiss.

"Didn't you miss this?" Her eyes shone with tears. "Maybe we don't have to be over, Shane. We were good together, weren't we?"

"Dana, don't do this."

She took a step away and folded her arms across her body. Her mouth bunched sideways into a pouty knot. "You're no fun anymore."

"I'm sorry you came all this way. I thought our FaceTime conversation made things clear."

"It did, I guess, but I wanted to see for myself if we're really over."

"You didn't come all the way across the pond for that, I'm sure."

"Well, I did." She clucked her tongue. "Okay, yes, I'm renting out my condo, and I had to sign some papers, meet the tenant, arrange for storage of my things, and all that. But seeing you was a priority, too, Shane. I had to see you."

"Dana, I appreciate that, I really do. But we can't let ourselves forget what got us here. We're on different roads. Don't you agree?"

"No." She fiddled with the scarf around her neck. "I don't know. Okay, yes, I suppose so."

He reached over and pulled her hand into his. "I

only want the best for you. And you're going to rock it in Milan."

A smile broke out across her mouth. "It's exciting."

He let go of her hand. "I wish you nothing but the best, Dana."

Her mouth turned downward. "It was a long way to come to officially say goodbye, I guess."

"I'm glad we had the chance to talk in person, then." He offered her a smile. "Milan agrees with you."

"*Grazie*." The compliment perked her up, and that flash returned to her gaze. "I do love it there." She tilted her head and eyed him. "Shane, we sure messed this up, didn't we?"

A wry smile curved his lips. "Not really. I think we just needed to admit we're two different people wanting two different things."

"And you've found someone that wants what you want, I gather."

It wasn't a question. She was stating a fact, only he didn't know how to respond without making matters worse. "Maybe we both have?"

She hadn't exactly said she was seeing someone new, but she might as well have. She had mentioned how *electric* it was when she was in the company of someone with similar life goals. That was one thing he and Dana could agree on. Spending time with Kit had proved the theory.

"Is there a chance you'll move there permanently?"

She shrugged. "There are variables. But for now, I'm on board for the rest of the year."

Shane wondered if one of those variables wore a Rolex. He simply nodded. "Good for you."

"And how about you after you complete the academy? When do you move into your apartment?"

Right now he couldn't imagine not waking up to the smell of coffee wafting out from the kitchen and sharing a cup with Kit before they started their mornings. The idea of leaving her place ticked at his insides like a kind of breakup. They were just getting started, and he did not want to let go.

"I just heard that my apartment's ready ahead of time. I could move in next week if I want to."

"Well." She gathered her purse and the sweater she had wrapped on the chairback. "I need to get some things done before I fly back. Thank you for dinner, Shane." She wrapped her arms around him. "Be happy."

"You too."

In a moment she was gone, and he was grateful they had had the chance to talk in person. Despite the business with her condo, it was a long way for her to come to say goodbye, but now he was glad she had. There were no regrets, no bitter feelings, and he was excited at the thought that his path to his future was free. He couldn't wait to see Kit.

On his way out of Jabberwocky's, he saw that he'd received a message on his phone. He slid a finger over the face of the device to reveal a text from his buddy Larry.

Hey. Just making sure you're okay. Never know when both your women show up at the same time. Give me a holler, Casanova.

His heart stalled. Both women? Had Kit come to Jabberwocky's tonight? What had she seen, or worse yet, what had she thought she'd seen? He didn't even take the time to respond to Larry's text. He hurried to his truck and drove straight home.

Chapter Thirty-Three

When he got to the house, his belongings were tossed onto the front stoop in a haphazard mound. His Mets throw was folded over the railing. His insides fell in on themselves.

The front door was locked, and when he inserted his key to open it, a chain stopped him. The deadbolt was on. *Shit.* Her car was there. She had to be home.

"Kit. Open the door." He pounded with his fist.

"Go away."

"Come on, Kit. Let's talk, please. Take off the deadbolt."

The door was cracked open, the lock's chain taut, and she peered into the space. "I don't want to talk. I don't want an explanation. I don't want to see you. Now, get your crap and get off my property."

"Not until you talk to me."

"I'm done talking."

"Don't do this, Kit. Please open the door."

"Oh, and you are relieved of your duty to accompany me to my cousin's wedding. I'm going alone."

"Alone? What are you going to tell everybody?"

"That we broke up. Simple. Show's over, Fireman."

"It hasn't been a show for a long time now, Kit. You know that."

"I know nothing."

He detected a catch in her voice, and it killed him to think he'd upset her this much. "Dana's gone. She and I had a talk and said our goodbyes."

"Please just go."

"Did you hear me?"

"I'm done listening to anything you say, Shane."

"But what about us?"

"Like I said, show's over."

"Nothing happened."

"Goodbye." She closed the door.

He knocked, but she did not respond. He didn't know how many minutes he stood there on the porch before he finally collected his belongings and carried them to his truck.

He took his phone out of his pocket and dialed Larry's number.

"How you doing, Irish?"

"What did you say to her?"

"Who?"

"Kit."

"Nothing really. I gave her my barstool when I was ready to leave."

"That's all?"

"I told her you were in the dining room with the other one. Did that make her mad?"

"I need a place to stay for a few days."

"I'm sorry, man."

Shane blew out a lungful of air. "It's not your fault, Larry. This is my doing, not yours. Can I bunk at your place?"

"Oh man, you went from two women to none. That's got to be a record."

Shane closed his eyes. "Can I come over?"

"Sure. No problem."

He ended the call and waited in his truck for a moment to see if by any miracle the front door would open. It did not. Finally, he started the engine and backed out of the driveway.

Chapter Thirty-Four

Shane carried in a change of clothes and his toiletries, walking past Larry at his open door. "Thanks."

"All I've got is the couch."

"That's all I need."

"How about a beer, too?"

They sipped their beers, sitting on the long couch that would later be made up as Shane's bed.

"My apartment is ready early." Shane took a swig. "They said I can move in as early as next Wednesday."

"Stay as long as you need, Irish. I feel like I'm partly responsible. So what happened anyway? Did the real girlfriend confront the pretend one?"

He groaned. "Please stop referring to them that way. Dana is the one who works in Milan."

"She's hot."

"And Kit's the one I'm renting a room from. Or at least I was."

"She's really hot, too." He whistled low. "Smoking."

He flashed him a look. "Seriously? Is that fireman talk? Describing women in terms of fire?"

Larry shrugged. "Ha, funny. But I couldn't help noticing, bro. I have eyes."

He shook his head and took another swig of his beer. "So in a nutshell, Dana and I are through. We've

213

been over, talked about it via FaceTime, but now we had the chance to say goodbye in person."

"She came all the way here from Europe to tell you that?"

"No. She's extending her time in Milan and is renting out her place and had some things to take care of. But as far as she and I are concerned, like I said, she and I already had a conversation about going in separate ways. But I think she got worked up about my moving on and took the chance to talk face-to-face. We ended on a good note, though."

"Is she one of those types who doesn't want you but doesn't want anybody else to have you?"

"I don't know. Maybe. Dana's got a hell of an ego, but she's a smart lady. She's got a lot going on, and she's thinking of making Italy a permanent thing."

"And where does the other one, um, Kit, fall into this?"

"I'm in love with her."

"You're what?"

"You heard me. I've fallen for her like a ton of bricks."

"How does she feel?"

"She hates me."

Larry shook his head. "We're going to have to get some more beer."

****

Kit paced through the rooms of her house while her mind spun with all the craziness that she'd lived since the day Shane Dugan showed up.

Rylee had told her to stay calm and hear Shane out when he came to explain. Well, she wasn't in the mood for any explanations. She'd seen what she'd seen. She was so pissed at him she could spit, but she was angrier with herself for taking a chance on him.

Damn Hop and his advice, too. *Believe and you'll achieve.* Such bullshit. Words like that worked when you were rock climbing or whatever spelunking was, but it wasn't meant for matters of the heart. At least not her heart. Her one overworked muscle. She was going to give it a rest, a good long one. A decade or two at least.

A tear slipped from her eye, and she swatted it. Damn him. Damn that fireman with his adorableness. She should have been smarter. But she'd be smarter now.

Now she had to face the wedding and telling everyone she and that man were over. Her mother would be upset, but she'd act as if it was all her idea to break up with the guy. It would be different from The Incident of last Christmas Eve. The world at large knew Brian had sideswiped her. Now at least, she could tell whatever tale about her breakup she wanted. There were no witnesses, and what was one more lie?

Chapter Thirty-Five

The day of the wedding was one of those spectacular July days saved for magical weddings for brides like Co-Co. The sun was bright, and the clouds in the sky, dotted here and there across the wide expanse of summer blue, looked as if an artist with generous dollops of white paint on his brush had placed the puffs just right.

Last night Kit had been given a reprieve from the rehearsal dinner. She'd had no business being there in the first place despite the bride's casual invite. She wasn't in the wedding, thank the Lord. But her mother was invited to the rehearsal, and Co-Co and her mother decided it would be "nice" if the person who'd turned their grandmother's gown into a "masterpiece" would be in attendance.

That would have meant needing to use the breakup story a day early. She just couldn't do it and face another day with all those people. That would have given everyone a chance to come up with pity remarks, and God only knew what that would have done to her mother's mood. However, lately her mother's favorite topic was the kitten named Smokey. She'd actually told Kit that after the rehearsal dinner, she'd gone over to Hop's to see the fluff ball. Thankfully, Mom hadn't popped in when she was in the midst of throwing Shane's belongings onto her stoop.

Her excuse for the rehearsal had been seamless. Claiming Shane needed to work was totally believable, and throwing in that she'd had to inspect some dresses at the shop had added to the nice tidy lie. As much as she hated spewing bullshit, she'd learned over these crazy weeks that sometimes it was necessary for survival's sake.

But now it was today—the wedding and the jig were up. She'd had it planned since yesterday, but this morning as she sat in her robe on the back deck, she called the river to speak to her, soothe her, give her strength. The worst part was she was still so full of lies, not just about telling her family that she and Shane were over. That story had been a falsehood from the start.

She took a sip of her tepid tea and closed her eyes when a breeze greeted her. The lie that sat heavy in her chest was the one she told herself when she'd said that it didn't matter, that kicking Shane out of her life and casting the man away were what she wanted and needed.

She missed him already. She was still capable of telling the truth, and it stung. She'd somehow put her faith in that fireman even when she'd thought her ability to trust was broken beyond repair. Being wrong about him had hurt her more than Brian's betrayal, and in truth, that part ached like her chest might split in half.

But she'd learned something else since Brian had hurt her. She learned that she'd survive. Time told her someday she wouldn't hurt so much about Shane. That had to be true because right now she couldn't breathe. She let the breeze whip through her hair and bathe her face, silently calling to the river with its reliable babble, willing it to speak to her. But all she heard was the rush of the water flowing over the rocks, the cadence all but chanting his name again and again. *Shane. Shane. Shane.*

****

The dress she had selected looked nice. It had been no picnic pulling all the size eights off the rack and eliminating them one by one based on how tight they were on her body. By the end of the exercise, she'd had two dresses to choose from.

Right now standing in front of the full-length mirror behind her door, she looked at her image. The bateau-necked navy sheath gave her a lean line, and it was roomy enough to give her comfort. But nothing would give her comfort today.

She'd agreed to meet the bride in the small holding room to make sure there were no last-minute stitching needs of the pretty, pretty princess before she made her grand entrance. She was glad that after today she and her needles and thread would be done with her cousin Co-Co. That was the one perk of this day.

Grabbing her purse, she gave herself one last look in the mirror. Lipstick in place, hair billowy and free, she left to go to the chapel where she'd lie to everyone in attendance. *Lordy.*

Chapter Thirty-Six

Cars lined the roadway outside the old chapel with the ancient stone façade. Kit loved the look of this place with the small bell tower jutting up like a beacon to all who entered. She swallowed hard as she navigated the flagstone walkway where tulle ribbons were tied into bows on the railings at the stairs.

A few attendees already sat in the wooden pews, although it was too early for the ceremony. The photographers—three of them, for God's sake—were setting up their equipment, and what appeared to be a planning person, a tallish woman with her hair in a too-tight bun, was fussing with the floral arrangements and the white fabric runner that had been rolled out onto the aisle.

The air inside the cavernous space was cool despite the heat outside. The organist up in the balcony played background music that Kit welcomed, the notes soothing and holy. An errant feeling of awe poured over her like water. Peace knocked on her broken heart and wanted in.

She found the small room where the bride awaited her. She opened the heavy door and stood in the entrance. Co-Co was in front of a wheeled, full-length mirror, most assuredly a piece of the bride's equipment.

Aunt Dee Dee looked lovely in her mauve taffeta suit with a peplum. Her hair was starched and choppy, and her earrings dangled, their swaying catching the glints of light coming in from the cross-hatched window.

But it was Co-Co who stole her breath. Gram's dress was spectacular on the bride's tiny frame. The fabric flowed as if it were alive, as if it had breath and a heart of its own. A tear stung the corner of Kit's eye.

"Kitty-Kat!" Co-Co opened her arms wide but did not move away from where she stood. Her maid of honor, Kelly, in a billowy yellow chiffon dress, stood at her side. Co-Co's face beamed, and Kit could not help but notice a quiver to the bride's perfectly glossed lips. "Well, what do you think, cousin? Do I do our grandmother's dress justice?"

With each step toward the bride, Kit willed the peace from the chapel to be with her. She licked her lips and blinked back the moisture in the corner of her eyes. "You're beautiful, Co-Co."

"You think so?"

Co-Co gently lifted the fabric into her hands and took a tiny yet giant step to stand before Kit. Her perfume, a springtime floral scent, wafted to Kit's nose. Her makeup was so perfectly applied she looked like a cover of a bridal magazine.

She grabbed Kit's hand. "Thank you." She paused and uttered a small nervous laugh. "Thank you for the magic you've done with this gown. It's perfect."

She nodded. "It is perfect."

"You look so pretty, Kit," Aunt Dee Dee cooed. "Your mother told me all about your dress, and she was right. You look like a movie star in it."

Kit emitted a noise that sounded like a laugh, but really, it was a release of air that had been trapped in her lungs. Mom had said she looked like a movie star? A lump grew in her throat. She swallowed hard.

Co-Co pressed her hands together, as if in prayer. "Mom, Kelly, will you excuse Kit and me for a moment?"

A pause hung heavy in the room, but her maid of honor broke the silence. "I'll go see how things are progressing out there."

"I've got to visit the powder room." Aunt Dee Dee took cautious steps across the wooden floor, hands up for balance, as if she were walking on ice. Maybe those two-inch sling backs weren't the best choice.

Kit's eyes lingered on the closed door after the bride's companions exited. She could feel Co-Co's stare from behind her.

"Kit…"

She turned her head. "I brought a needle and thread if we need it. Is everything okay with the dress?" Moving into seamstress mode was like shrugging into a favorite old coat. She stepped around Co-Co and examined the back of the dress. She touched her fingers to the fabric-covered buttons. She knew without counting there were thirty-seven. "The buttons are secure."

Co-Co covered Kit's hand. "I want to say something, Kitty-Kat. Please let me."

She didn't want to hear whatever her cousin had to say. Despite its brokenness, her heart thudded in her chest, and she feared that muscle could not take one more tugging before it fell to pieces like a bad game of Jenga.

"This is your day, Co-Co."

She squeezed Kit's hand. "You've been wonderful

through this, cousin. I know how selfish I've been." A nervous laugh came from her lips. "Since forever, right? I mean, you've had to deal with me and my antics since we were in kindergarten." She smiled, and that tremble was back on her lips in a discernible quiver.

Kit's heart squeezed. *Don't. Please don't.*

But the bride continued. "I was delighted when I learned you and Shane were so happy. Really that was more selfishness on my part, wasn't it? If you're happy, then I can rest easy with what happened with Brian and my being together." A caustic laugh popped from her mouth. "But don't think I don't know in here how much I've hurt you." She closed her fist and held it to the place where her heart beat. "And that's the price, Kit. I'll always know."

Kit pulled in a breath and expelled. "Co-Co, it's your wedding day. How you and your groom came to be doesn't matter now. True love is true love. Right?"

"You wanted Grammy's gown. I knew it all along."

"Yes, I did."

"Yet you helped make it look like this." She gently lifted her arms wide, like a bird about to take flight. "You've made me beautiful."

"You were born beautiful."

"Not inside. Not always."

"Gram would be proud of you now."

A tear dribbled down the bride's cheek. "Mostly of you, Kitty-Kat. You and Grammy were cut from the same cloth. Both of you funny and likeable, everyone clamoring to be around you to hear what you've got to say about any old thing. And like you, she was smart and nice. Really nice. Everyone wanted to be like her." She swatted at the tear that had dribbled down her face just in time for another one to cascade down the other cheek. "To be like you."

Instinctively Kit reached up and stopped the tear from traveling to Co-Co's chin. They locked gazes as her finger froze where it touched the bride's face. "Look at you messing with that makeup," she admonished. "Stop now, Co-Co. Where's your makeup? Let's touch you up."

"On the table."

Kit went to the table and opened what looked like an overnight bag. She withdrew a compact of powder and a brush. "Is this the brush you use for the powder?" She came up to Co-Co with the brush aimed.

"Yes, but, Kit…"

"Close your eyes and your mouth, too."

Co-Co did as she was told, and Kit tapped the brush into the powder, blew off the excess, and gently dabbed it over her cousin's expertly applied makeup.

"You know—"

"Stop talking for crying out loud, Co-Co."

A smile turned up on Co-Co's mouth. "You're not the boss of me."

The words conjured all the times over the years when the two girls had locked horns. Kit had always been the wronged one, and Co-Co the perpetrator of some sneaky or underhanded escapade. She studied her cousin's face as she stood there with her chin up and her eyes closed. The false lashes were expertly applied and looked like dark fans feathering out from her eyes. Kit bit down on her lip. Had she been pompous over all this time, knowing she was the self-proclaimed good one, the nice cousin? Had that given her the kind of satisfaction Co-Co had gotten from her own antics? What did it matter now? This young woman was about to embark on her new life, and today of all days this tearful bride wanted Kit to know she was sorry and had even confessed that she'd wished she were more like her.

"Good as new," Kit said.

Co-Co opened her eyes. "Thank you, cousin."

"You're welcome." They shared a smile.

The door opened, and Kelly and Aunt Dee Dee came in with their cousin Paul, dapper in his tuxedo. Outside the doorway, music met her ears. The organist was playing the "Bridal Chorus."

"Look at you," Paul gushed, and just the sound of his awe brought another stinging tear to Kit's eyes.

She needed to get a grip. She stepped away and made her way toward the door.

Kelly did a little hop and flashed a grin. "Kit, your man's out there already."

My man? "Shane?"

"Of course Shane, silly. He looks delicious in that dark suit. Hubba-hubba."

Shane was here at the ceremony?

"I, um, better get out there." She turned to the bride, who was fussing with her bouquet. They shared a wink.

"He's sitting with your mom up in the second row."

She went through the door and slowly walked to the chapel, trying to remember how to breathe.

Chapter Thirty-Seven

She made her way to the second row in the now-filled chapel and fixed her gaze on the interaction between Shane and her mother. Shane's head was tucked low as he spoke to Mom in a whisper that the atmosphere called for. Her mother's well-coiffed, still-unsettling red head bobbed in agreement with whatever that two-timing fireman was saying to her. Her chest constricted as she tapped the shoulder of the man on the end of the aisle, and he stood to allow Kit's access to the pew.

"Hello, darling, you look wonderful." Her mother squeezed her shoulders in a scrunch of delight. "Doesn't she, Shane? Doesn't Kit look divine?"

Out of necessity, she let her gaze filter to him. His eyes were locked on her, the green in them dark in the subdued lighting of the chapel. A rueful smile claimed his mouth.

"I couldn't agree more," he said. "Kit, you're beautiful."

"Why are you here?" Her whisper was acidic.

"I had to."

She turned away from him. There was no point in fixing it now. She'd have to lower the boom eventually that she and Shane were done. But not now. Not in this place. She adjusted herself to sit between her mother and Shane.

She cast her gaze to the front of the room, and there he was—Brian in a tuxedo, looking as if he belonged on the top of a triple-tiered cake. He fidgeted with the black-satin bow tie at his neck. He was handsome in his finery, but it amazed her how the animosity she'd felt was gone today. He could be a stranger or an actor portraying a groom on a celluloid screen. For that she was grateful. Now she was busy trying to ignore the man seated beside her.

Shane reached over and placed a program on her lap. "I got one of these for you."

Flustered by the feel of his hand on her leg, she fought to not flinch. There would be time later to address this man. She looked down at the pamphlet as she worked to still her mind.

"There's a nice tribute to you inside," he offered.

"What?"

"Read it."

She glanced down at the cover with the names of the bride and groom in a fancy scripted font. She turned the page to read a listing of all the people involved in the ceremony, the attendants, the parents, the two flower girls, and the family friend who would be doing a reading from scripture. Then at the bottom of the page, she saw her name.

A special thank you to Kit Baxter, cousin of the bride, for her expertise in turning their grandmother's wedding gown, a prized family heirloom, into a modern, spectacular dream dress. You make dreams come true.

She lifted her gaze to meet Shane's.

"Looks like you've made quite an impression on the bride, huh?"

"Impressions can be false." She turned away.

"I was giving you one more minute."

Kit turned to her mother's words. And although she was sure all this tension was making her hallucinate, there was Hop Monaco inching past people in their pew to take a seat beside her mother. He wore a charcoal-gray suit, and his tie, a riot of paisley, was crooked.

He sat between Kit and her mother. She heard him give his excuse to Mom. "There was no parking out there. I was doing laps around the block."

Her mother didn't look at him, just fanned herself, like a debutante, with her program. "That's what happens when you're late."

"Better late than never, Red."

From the corner of her eye, Kit saw her mother turn to him. Her mouth was in a full ear-to-ear grin. She angled her head in a coy tilt. "Time will tell, old man."

Kit elbowed him. Her whisper was hot. "What are you doing here?"

"I'm Regina's date." He shrugged. "How's that grab ya?"

She wondered what Shane was thinking but forced herself not to turn toward him.

The procession began with Brian's mother being ushered down the aisle by one of the groomsmen. Kit knew the guy. He was one of Brian's college friends who she'd come to know when she had been dating him. Brian's mom wore a lacy pearl-gray gown with a cowl neckline. She looked happy and proud, regal even.

"She looks lovely." Mom leaned over Hop's lap and whispered to her as Brian's mom passed their pew. "But the dye on her shoes is too dark."

"Mom," she said.

"I have an eye for color, that's all."

The comment made Hop chuckle.

The rest of the bridal party paraded in, and then everyone stood. The bride appeared, and a gasp sounded in unison in the room. She slowly navigated the aisle on the arm of Paul, their steps in precision. Co-Co beamed. Everything Kit had ever thought of her cousin had stilled in this moment, frozen in time for some other day. Gram's dress shone like gossamer wings under the candlelight, and a sense of pride warmed Kit in the center of her chest. The bride cast an appreciative glance to Kit as she passed by their pew.

"You did such a wonderful job on the gown," her mother whispered. She reached across Hop, placed a hand over Kit's, and gave it a squeeze.

"Thanks, Mom."

The ceremony went on, and Kit fought to pay attention against the whirlwind in her mind. All the things that had happened leading up to this wedding spun around and around so fast that one moment bled into another as the details ramped up the velocity. Air was thin in such a vortex.

A touch to her shoulder startled her. She turned toward Shane.

"You okay?"

"Of course."

He offered a reassuring smile.

Go away.

The friend scheduled to do a reading made her way up to the pulpit, and Kit forced herself to concentrate. The woman spoke all the things that love was and what it was not. Kit sat up straighter, pressing her back against the cool wood of the pew. She let the words bathe her with their talk of love's patience and its honor, how love was not a scorekeeper and had nothing to do with envy or holding on to anger. Love, she continued, rejoiced with truth, and the words cemented in her head and in her heart. They evaporated the whirlwind in her mind, leaving her with a calmness she hadn't felt in days. She felt Shane's eyes on her, but she would not turn toward him.

****

After the ceremony Kit and her mother waited for the valet to deliver her car. Shane came up to stand beside her.

"I'll meet you over there," he said to the two of them. When she did not respond, he came in close. "Please let me talk with you for a minute. Please."

She plastered on a fake smile. "No, thank you."

Gripping her elbow, he leaned closer to Mom and told her they'd be right back. Then he steered her toward the door.

She shot a hot whisper. "What are you doing? My car's coming."

"One minute. Just give me one minute."

"No."

They stopped, and he pulled her hands into his. For the sake of those coming and going around them, she did not yank free.

"Kit, what you saw at Jabberwocky's was me and Dana saying goodbye. She came back for just a couple of days to finalize some things with her condo and took the time to come see me."

"To say goodbye."

"Not at first. At first she tried to convince me that she and I might be able to make a go of it."

"I'll bet."

"But…" He touched her face. "Look at me, Kit. But I was truthful with her. It's been over for a long time, and we agreed to wish each other well. That's what you saw."

His eyes, the green so bright now in the sunlight, looked true and honest. She almost told him she believed him. But there were too many lies swirling in her head from all the ones they'd been telling that she couldn't think.

"Kit, honey, the car is here."

Her mother stood at the sidewalk next to her lease, the front doors open, awaiting them.

"I have to go."

And she walked away.

****

On the way over to the restaurant with her mother, she tried to sort out the things Shane had just said. Her head spun.

Hop had wanted to take his own truck to the reception and had given Regina a smirky look before he left them on the sidewalk outside the chapel. "Don't get into any trouble while I'm gone."

Mom's response was a playful push to his chest. "You're the only trouble I'm dealing with right now, you old coot."

Mom adjusted herself on the faux-leather seat. "Why is your Shane driving by himself to the reception, honey?"

"Um…" She could tell her mother right now. They were all alone in the car, no one else to hear her awful truth. But if she told Mom now that Shane and she were never a couple in the first place, she'd have to face the aftermath during the entire reception. She was reminded of the words quoted in the reading at the chapel—how truth was the way, truly the only way. Yet it would be just as easy to say he was on call with the fire department, how handy. But that would be just one more blasted lie.

A new tack bought her time. "Mom, first you want to tell me what Hop's doing here as your date?"

Her mother waved a dismissive hand. "I must have rocks in my head. That's why."

"I don't understand. I thought you detested the man."

"I probably still do. Who knows?" Mom laughed and touched a gentle hand to her hair. "But, boy, does that man make me laugh. And he just loves my new color, and I get a charge out of him calling me *Red*. To think a little, lost kitten turned us into friends, or what's that they call it? Oh yes, frenemies."

Kit stared through the windshield as she processed her mother's newfound connection to Hop. It was a confession of sorts. Now it was her turn.

"So, Mom, there's something I need to say."

Her mother turned to her, her mouth set. "Is this about your grandmother's wedding gown, Kitrina?"

"What?"

"Gram's dress. I know you wanted it for your own wedding someday. But…"

"No, Mom. It's not about the dress."

"Are you sure? Because if it is, there's something I'd like to tell you about that. The gown wasn't Gram's first wedding dress."

She gripped the steering wheel. "Not her first dress. What are you talking about?"

Mom waved a hand. "It's a big family secret because back in the day anything out of the so-called norm was taboo. It's time somebody told the truth."

Kit turned into the banquet hall's lot and pulled up to the valet stand. An attendant helped her mother from the vehicle, and as Kit exited, she handed the car key to a driver. Her heart pounded. What was the truth her mother was about to reveal? Here she'd thought she was the only one with a secret today.

Inside the plush lobby she and her mom stepped over to the side while guests continued to arrive. A server came by with a tray of champagne flutes where whole strawberries bobbed in the fizzy liquid. She and her mom each reached for a glass at the same time.

When the server walked away, she turned to her mother. "Okay, you want to explain what you meant by what you just said, Mother?"

"Okay, but if you tell anybody about this, I'll have to kill you, which would be such a shame because I'm so fond of you."

She smiled. "Pinky swear."

"Okay." Her mother leaned in. "Do you remember when you told me that your cousin was going to wear your grandmother's gown and you were feeling upset about it?"

"Yes."

"Well, do you remember what I said to you then?"

Kit wracked her brain. She remembered the day. They had been at Aunt Dee Dee's house for the family meet-and-greet. She and Mom had stolen away into the library down the hallway. It was when Mom told her she never thought she and Brian were good for each other. But what had she said about the dress?

Mom clucked her tongue. "I told you that it was just fabric sewn into a dress."

She did remember that but had chalked it up to more of her mother attempting to keep the peace within the family.

"Okay, yes, I remember."

"It wasn't the dress that blessed my mother and father's marriage. It was the two people that they were. Remember my saying that?"

"Yes, but what's that got to do with that not being her first wedding gown?"

"My parents eloped when my mother was just eighteen."

"What?"

"Lower your voice, would you? This is top secret."

"Seriously? Top secret? That's seems a bit dramatic."

"Are you kidding?" Her mother put a hand to her chest. "To the rules of this family back in the forties, what my parents did was so unrefined they may as well have run down Main Street naked."

Kit couldn't help it. She laughed. "Does Aunt Dee Dee know?"

"Of course she knows, but no one else."

"Mom, that's crazy. They eloped. They didn't kill someone."

"Your grandmother's family on my father's side was a bunch of starched shirts, and I know I've been the same way in some respects. But the times they are a-changing." Mom's eyes warmed. "How silly now to think it was scandalous for a young girl to elope with a soldier. My father was getting shipped out to Okinawa, and they wanted to be married before he left, so they sneaked off to town hall. My grandparents forbade their daughter to marry in that manner, but my mother did it anyway."

"Go, Gram."

"Yes, I understand that now. Go, Gram. And ever since this whole thing with Brian and Co-Co, I fell into that hush-hush, shove-it-under-the-carpet nonsense. But hell, it's a new day, and you're the one who's so much like my mother. Your cousin got the gown, but you've got the woman alive in your soul."

She choked back a tear. "Mom, where's this coming from?"

Mom lifted one coy shoulder. "I'm seeing things a bit differently these days, that's all."

"So Gram kept a lie going."

"Gram didn't tell her parents the truth until my father made it home safe and sound. They insisted she have a quote, unquote real wedding, a full-blown marriage in their church officiated by their longtime pastor, the whole shebang. I'd call it self-preservation rather than a lie."

Kit swallowed hard. *Oh, Gram. We had more in common than I knew.*

Mom smiled as she winked. "So she got married her way first. That's what counts."

"Wow, Mom. That's something."

Her mother flashed a sly look, and a teasing light came into her eyes. "And I'm in possession of Gram's dress from that visit to the justice of the peace."

Suddenly she knew, and her heart did a whirl. "The pearly-pink dress with the rhinestone buckle."

Mom nodded. "And no one's getting their paws on that one but you, my love. That one's for you."

A tear tumbled down her cheek. "I'll cherish it."

"Now go find your man."

"About that, Mom. I have a confession."

"Okay."

"He and I were never really a couple. He's a friend of Hop's, a new recruit to the fire department. He needed a room to rent temporarily, and I needed money because that old tree demolished my Honda. So Shane moved into my loft and paid me up front so I could lease a car."

"But I don't understand, honey. Why'd you tell everybody he was your beau?"

"It's a long story, but Co-Co was in Rosie's with Gram's gown, Shane came in to discuss the idea of renting the loft, and Co-Co and Aunt Dee Dee assumed he was my new man. Overhearing the moving-in discussion, they thought we were moving in together."

"And you let them believe it."

"Because it was easier."

Her mother nodded. "Self-preservation, my love."

"Yes."

"So when did things change then, honey? When did your heart get involved?"

"How'd you know?"

"A mother knows. You love each other."

"It's complicated."

"Life is complicated."

"I think it may be over, Mom. I thought he could still have feelings for his former girlfriend."

"What makes you say so?"

"I saw them in an embrace. He swears it was just a goodbye, but I shut down on him and won't let him explain. Mom, I can't go through something like that again."

"First off, give yourself a break. It's like if you ever got caught in a house fire, you can't help but think you smell smoke where there's none. But you can't let one man's behavior scare you away from another. At least hear the boy out."

Maybe. She looked around for him.

"Go find him, Kit, but first let's toast." Her mother lifted her glass, and so did Kit.

"To the one you can't live without and doing it your own way."

Kit sipped her champagne.

"Oh, look." Mom smiled. "There's Shane."

Chapter Thirty-Eight

In a flurry of arrivals, Kit's mother slipped away
and headed to the ladies' room with Aunt Dee Dee, and
Kit seized the chance to talk with Shane. She'd been so
angry earlier, but now after her talk with her mother,
the anger had morphed into sadness. She studied his
face and realized she loved him despite what she'd seen
in the restaurant when Dana had come back from
Milan. Maybe she had been too quick to judge what
she'd seen. Maybe it was too close to the scene she'd
lived through with Brian and Co-Co. Her mind was a
jumble; her heart quickened in her chest. Maybe it was
the champagne on an empty stomach.

His eyes were on her as she closed the distance
between them. "Shane, look—"

"Please just listen, Kit."

"But—"

"Please."

She closed her mouth and waited.

"I know how it had to have looked, but when I
came home to explain, you had locked me out. That's
how things get more messed up."

The way he said *home* made her heart fall. She
missed him being up in the loft, missed seeing him in
the morning over a cup of coffee and discussing the day
ahead.

"Tell me you believe me."

"Kit!"

She turned to Co-Co's signature high-pitched tone. She clutched her oversized bouquet and trotted over to them. She grabbed Kit's arm. "Come on. We're taking a picture with our mothers." She turned her attention to Shane. "Hi, you. Don't you look delicious."

"Congratulations, Co-Co."

"Come on, Kit. They're waiting."

She left Shane there in the lobby while she allowed the bride to whisk her up the grand staircase where their mothers waited with a photographer. The man positioned the four of them on the top step and then repositioned them until he finally decided he had the right angle.

While he fussed, Aunt Dee Dee leaned in around her daughter to speak to Kit. "Thank you one more time for what you've done with my mother's wedding gown."

Her mother gave Kit's back a squeeze as she stood close.

"All right, ladies, stand tall and smile."

Kit felt her lips curve into a smile, but her eyes cast beyond the photographer in search of Shane. Maybe he was a man of honor, as he vowed, as her heart now dared to hope. Her heart fluttered in a series of clicks to the sound of the photographer's rapid finger on his camera taking shot after shot. Hope bloomed fuller with each second and dared to pound a message of the truth she believed to her soul—there was nothing "maybe" about Shane Dugan.

Chapter Thirty-Nine

Kit dashed to the reception room, passing through the slow-moving throng of those finding their seats. She consulted her seat card, table four. No one was there yet, chairs empty, place settings sparkling and untouched.

She surveyed the room. No Shane. She hoped he hadn't given up and left.

She backtracked to the bar and peered through the doorway where guests were gathered. She elbowed her way through the clusters of people.

"Looking for someone?"

She turned to the voice. Brian.

"Oh, hi. Um, congratulations, Brian."

"Thank you. You look great, Kit, by the way."

"Thank you."

A heavy pause hung in the air between them.

"Are you happy, Kit?"

I hope so. I hope it's not too late to convince Shane I believe him.

"I don't think it should take that long to answer the question." Brian's eyes danced with that superiority he liked to flaunt. He chugged whatever brown liquid was in his short square glass. "I've got to go in there and try to remember my dance steps." He made a face. "The things we do for love."

Yes! Love made you do crazy things.

She tilted her head and offered him a smile. "Be happy, Brian. Take care of my cousin. Now I need to find Shane."

Her cell phone vibrated in her small purse, and she withdrew the device and connected the call.

"Hey, kid."

"Hi, Hop. You okay?"

"Of course I'm okay. Why wouldn't I be okay?"

"Oh, I don't know. You could be having another crisis. Like maybe you found another kitten or something." His chuckle in her ear made her grin. She loved the old guy.

"Are you always a wise guy?"

"Not always. Just with you."

"Ha ha. Listen, where's your mother? I looked everywhere but the ladies' room. She hiding on me?"

"We were just taking pictures on the stairs. Everyone's going in for dinner."

"Oh, okay. Did Shane find you?"

"He did, but our conversation got interrupted. I was just about to go find him."

"I warned him, you know. From day one I warned him."

"Warned him about what?"

Hop blew out a whoosh of air. "About you. I told him not to fall for you because you were trouble with a capital *T*."

"I am not."

"Yeah, okay."

"Is that all, old man?"

"No. I called to tell you that boy's one good kid. He's honest and smart. Tomorrow when he accepts his certificate at the fire academy, I'm going to be there to hand it to him. The new regime said Irish requested me. That's what kind of man he is. Loyal."

"That's wonderful, Hop."

"You're going to be there, aren't you?"

"I wouldn't miss it."

He chuckled. "Red's coming, too. How about that."

"How about that." She smiled against the device she held to her ear. Mom and Hop. Who knew?

"Oh yeah," he said. "Wait till you see my new toy, kid."

"What'd you get?"

"A camper. A honey of a camper. Going to do it, Kit. Going to have an adventure."

"Good for you, Hop." A tear stung her eye. "I'm so glad for you."

"And if I play my cards right, that pain-in-the-ass mother of yours might be coming along with me."

Mom in a camper? Her brain couldn't wrap around that idea, but it made her chuckle.

"What about Smokey?"

"You're going to watch him. You owe me, remember."

"That's a deal."

"Hey, I see your mother. I've got to go. Oh cripes, wait till you hear this—she's even got me dancing."

****

Kit stood at the entrance of the ballroom. The band played a familiar old favorite from the Sinatra era, and the bride and groom danced in the center of the parquet dance floor. Other couples danced around them, all taking the same measured steps, their movements in unison. Hop and Mom kind of swayed side-to-side but didn't actually go anywhere. Now and then Mom lifted her head and laughed with her mouth open.

Her eyes found Shane. On the edge of the dance floor, one foot on the parquet, the other on the dark blue carpeting, he danced with Abigail in her flower-girl dress, and she looked up at him, eyes wide, broad grin cutting across her face. They ignored the other dancers and made their own steps. He twirled Abigail, and she pirouetted as she'd promised, moving as she'd learned in dance class with one arm held gracefully in the air. Kit's heart squeezed and expanded in her chest. That was Shane—spontaneous, taking his own steps, no calculations, moving with the flow. She loved him.

She made her way across the room as the music changed to a faster, upbeat song with a lot of percussion. Most of the choreographed dancers left the dance floor and went back to their seats. Abigail dashed off at her mother's call, and Shane made his way across the dance floor.

She squared her shoulders and stepped toward him, her heels clicking on the parquet. He stopped and stared at her.

"Care to dance?" she asked. "I'm not much of a dancer, but I'd like to try."

He tilted his head, the one side of his mouth curving up into a half smile. "All you have to do is go with it."

"A wise man once told me all you had to do was let yourself feel it."

He slipped his arms around her waist. Being in his arms was like coming home, and she pressed closer. He swayed left and then swayed right. His words came out in a whisper. "And do you, Kit? Do you feel it?"

She held his gaze. She placed a hand to her own

chest. "I feel it here." She kissed him. "I love you, Fireman."

He tucked his head and whispered so close it tickled her ear. "I love you, Kit. Only you. For now and for always."

"I can't believe this has happened. This is crazy." She laughed to keep the tears that filled her eyes from falling.

"It is. But I have something even crazier to say. Ready?"

Maybe. No. Screw maybe.

She uttered a breathless "Yes."

"Okay. Kit Baxter, one of these days I'm going to marry you."

A smile claimed her lips. "And when that happens, I'll be wearing a pink dress with a rhinestone buckle."

He laughed. "That I gotta see."

"Oh, you will, Shane. You will."

And she fell into step with the music, aware yet uncaring that she didn't know what the heck she was doing with her feet. The only direction she needed was there in the green eyes of her fireman.

A word about the author…

Born to a feisty Italian mother and a gentle blue-eyed Irishman, multi-award-winning author M. Kate Quinn draws on her quirky sense of humor, hopelessly romantic nature, highly developed sense of family and friendship, and her love for a good story while writing her novels.

Her books have won and placed in such contests as The Golden Quill Award, a win and a subsequent final for the Golden Leaf Award, and the Heart of Excellence Readers Choice Award.

Her next project, The Sycamore River Series, is a trilogy of romances set in a quaint New Jersey town, the first installment, *Saying Yes to the Mess*, released August 2018.

M. Kate Quinn, a lifelong native of New Jersey, makes her home in Central Jersey with her husband, where they enjoy big raucous gatherings with their large family and three amazing grandchildren.

Thank you for purchasing
this publication of The Wild Rose Press, Inc.

For questions or more information
contact us at
info@thewildrosepress.com.

The Wild Rose Press, Inc.
www.thewildrosepress.com

To visit with authors of
The Wild Rose Press, Inc.
join our yahoo loop at
http://groups.yahoo.com/group/thewildrosepress/